The Trouble with Crushes

By:
Brooke St. James

Published in Nashville, Tennessee, by Elm Hill, an imprint of Thomas Nelson. Elm Hill and Thomas Nelson are registered trademarks of HarperCollins Christian Publishing, Inc.

Elm Hill titles may be purchased in bulk for educational, business, fund-raising, or sales promotional use. For information, please e-mail SpecialMarkets@ThomasNelson.com.

ISBN 978-1-40033-3004

Other titles available from Brooke St. James:

Another Shot:
(A Modern-Day Ruth and Boaz Story)

When Lightning Strikes

Something of a Storm (All in Good Time #1)
Someone Someday (All in Good Time #2)

Finally My Forever (Meant for Me #1)
Finally My Heart's Desire (Meant for Me #2)
Finally My Happy Ending (Meant for Me #3)

Shot by Cupid's Arrow

Dreams of Us

Meet Me in Myrtle Beach (Hunt Family #1)
Kiss Me in Carolina (Hunt Family #2)
California's Calling (Hunt Family #3)
Back to the Beach (Hunt Family #4)
It's About Time (Hunt Family #5)

Loved Bayou (Martin Family #1)
Dear California (Martin Family #2)
My One Regret (Martin Family #3)
Broken and Beautiful (Martin Family #4)
Back to the Bayou (Martin Family #5)

Almost Christmas

JFK to Dublin (Shower & Shelter Artist Collective #1)
Not Your Average Joe (Shower & Shelter Artist Collective #2)
So Much for Boundaries (Shower & Shelter Artist Collective #3)
Suddenly Starstruck (Shower & Shelter Artist Collective #4)
Love Stung (Shower & Shelter Artist Collective #5)
My American Angel (Shower & Shelter Artist Collective #6)

Summer of '65 (Bishop Family #1)
Jesse's Girl (Bishop Family #2)
Maybe Memphis (Bishop Family #3)
So Happy Together (Bishop Family #4)
My Little Gypsy (Bishop Family #5)
Malibu by Moonlight (Bishop Family #6)
The Harder They Fall (Bishop Family #7)
Come Friday (Bishop Family #8)
Something Lovely (Bishop Family #9)

So This is Love (Miami Stories #1)
All In (Miami Stories #2)
Something Precious (Miami Stories #3)

The Suite Life (The Family Stone #1)
Feels Like Forever (The Family Stone #2)
Treat You Better (The Family Stone #3)
The Sweetheart of Summer Street (The Family Stone #4)
Out of Nowhere (The Family Stone #5)

Delicate Balance (Blair Brothers #1)
Cherished (Blair Brothers #2)
The Whole Story (Blair Brothers #3)
Dream Chaser (Blair Brothers #4)

Kiss & Tell (Novella) (Tanner Family #0)
Mischief & Mayhem (Tanner Family #1
Reckless & Wild (Tanner Family #2)
Heart & Soul (Tanner Family #3)
Me & Mister Everything (Tanner Family #4)
Through & Through (Tanner Family #5)
Lost & Found (Tanner Family #6)
Sparks & Embers (Tanner Family #7)
Young & Wild (Tanner Family #8)

Easy Does It (Bank Street Stories #1)
The Trouble with Crushes (Bank Street Stories #2)
A King for Christmas (Novella) (A Bank Street Christmas)
Diamonds Are Forever (Bank Street Stories #3)
Secret Rooms and Stolen Kisses (Bank Street Stories #4)
Feels Like Home (Bank Street Stories #5)
Just Like Romeo and Juliet (Bank Street Stories #6)
See You in Seattle (Bank Street Stories #7)
The Sweetest Thing (Bank Street Stories #8)
Back to Bank Street (Bank Street Stories #9)

Split Decision (How to Tame a Heartbreaker #1)
B-Side (How to Tame a Heartbreaker #2)

Cole for Christmas

Somewhere in Seattle (Alexander Family #1)

CHAPTER 1

Abigail Cohen
Galveston Island, Texas
August 1972

*M*y sister, Tess, had been living in Galveston for the last four years, and in that time, I had lived there twice and visited a lot. It was a lovely island community on the gulf shore of Texas, and it was only a few hours from the small town in Louisiana where we grew up.

I lived with her during the summer of '68 when she first moved there. And then two years later, after I finished college, I moved to Galveston again and stayed for a year. This time, I was with my boyfriend, Albert.

That hadn't ended well. I left Galveston after we broke up, which was a little over a year ago. Since then, I had been back at home in Starks where I worked as an elementary school teacher.

I was just about to go into my second year of teaching first grade. It was late August, and we were about to start back to school.

I was currently in Galveston, though. I had been there for over a week. I didn't want to leave, so I was pushing it on getting back to Starks. I had a teachers' meeting tomorrow morning, so I had no choice but to head back home tonight. I needed to go back, anyway, so that I could prepare for the school year and get my lesson plans ready.

I would leave Galveston tonight, but I was extremely reluctant about it. Not only was I in love with this city, but my big sister, Tess, was about to have a baby any day. That was the main reason why I had pushed back my trip as much as possible. Tess and Billy were having a baby, and it was due four days ago.

I had come to town to throw her a baby shower, which happened last weekend. I planned on her having the baby on time or a little early, but it turned out that due dates were just a guess, and there we were with me waiting until the last minute to get back for school.

I had really hoped to be there when my niece or nephew was born. That's not to say that I couldn't still make that happen once I went back home. Starks was only a couple of hours from Galveston, and I knew I would leave at the drop of a hat once he or she was born. That was what my parents were planning on doing. But I had my head wrapped around meeting the munchkin while I was there for the week, and it felt weird going home before it happened.

At the moment, I was sitting at a table at Carson's Diner with my very pregnant sister. This restaurant was at the end of a city block that felt like home to me—Bank Street between 23rd and 24th. The apartment Tess and I rented was on the corner of 23rd and Bank, and the diner was across Bank and on the corner of 24th. In between those places were familiar businesses and buildings, including the hardware store and Bank Street Boxing.

Tess and Billy had gotten married and stayed in that apartment for a few years after I moved out. They had only recently moved into their own home which was still on Bank Street but five blocks down, on the corner of 17th.

They still came down to this part of Bank Street all the time after they moved, though. Billy was a professional boxer who trained in the building next door to the diner and across the street from the hardware store where Tess used to work.

Billy was now a champion boxer with multiple titles, so he was at the gym full-time, and Tess went to see him there a few times throughout any given week. She continued to come even after she got pregnant and quit working at the hardware store.

We knew all of the business owners and neighbors, so even though they had moved out of the apartment, this block was still home to Tess and Billy. It felt a bit like home to me, too, though I technically hadn't lived there since that first summer.

I took comfort in the familiar sights and sounds of the diner on the corner. It was predictably busy in there, and today's lunch crowd was no different than usual. The diner was more than half-full with only a few open tables or booths. My order was predictable also—a club sandwich with potato chips. Betty was still working there as a waitress and she knew I liked extra bacon instead of ham on my club sandwich. They always made it right at Carson's. We had already ordered, but the food hadn't arrived at our table yet. Somebody had put money in the jukebox, and a song by Elvis was playing in the background.

"There's Ms. Nancy," Tess said, looking over my shoulder toward the door. I turned to look that way. "She doesn't see us," Tess added.

I caught a glimpse of Nancy King coming in the door before I turned back around. I really didn't know her that well. I knew her son, Daniel, really well, but I hadn't spent much time with his mom. She was the type of person who was so happy and put-together that it was intimidating. She was pretty and young-looking for having two grown children. She was married to a successful business owner with a perfect family— two kids, a boy and a girl. She was one of those people who just managed to do it all. I liked her, don't get me wrong. She had been nothing but nice to me. It's just that I was a little intimidated by her.

"Daniel just got out of the Army," Tess said.

I nodded absentmindedly. "I heard Billy talking about it the other day."

My heart ached when she mentioned Daniel King. He was such a sweet guy who had been thrown into a world of war and violence in Vietnam.

"What are you thinking about?" Tess asked, seeing me get lost in thought.

"Daniel," I said. "I hope he's okay. I hope he's not hurt or anything."

"He did get hurt," Tess said. "That was part of him getting that award."

"What award?"

"I don't know. Some big deal. I think it was a Purple Heart or the Medal of Honor. I haven't seen Ms. Nancy in a little while. Billy was telling me about it."

"I knew he'd be a hero," I said. "I'm so happy he's okay."

"Then why do you sound so sad about it?" she asked.

She was right. I did sound sad. "I don't know. I was just thinking, and I feel sad about him. Regret, I guess. I talked to him a lot when he first left home, but I should have been there for him more in the last couple of years. He probably had it hard over there, and I'm sure he needed a lot more support than I gave him. It's just that I had finished college, and I was looking for a job, and I had moved... and... Albert and everything."

"Was that when you quit talking to Daniel?" Tess asked. "I didn't even know you talked to him for that long."

I nodded. "Yeah. We kept in touch for two years when he first left."

"Doing what?" she asked.

"What do you mean, doing what?"

"Were you writing letters? Talking on the phone?"

"Writing letters," I said. "He wrote me twice a week like clockwork, but I missed sometimes. They're real regimented over there. I think he had certain days and times when he sat down and did correspondence."

"Two letters a week? I didn't know you guys talked that much," Tess said, looking at me like she was genuinely curious. "I thought you were dating someone in Lake Charles before Albert."

"I was. Daniel and I are just friends. The guys I dated in college didn't even care about Daniel. They didn't even know about him. It was just letters. And it's not like we talked about getting married or me waiting for him or anything."

"Yeah, but twice a week is a lot. I had no idea. When did you stop?"

"Two years ago, when I moved into that house with Albert. You know how jealous Albert was. He saw my mail and he didn't want Daniel sending me stuff, even if he was just my friend. He made me tell him to stop writing."

Betty, our waitress walked up to our table right then. She set our drinks in front of us. She said something about our order being out in just a minute.

We thanked her, and I smiled, but I was lost in thought, remembering how it had all gone down with me telling Daniel we couldn't correspond anymore. I got a flash of a memory of a phone conversation I had with him. He had called when he got the letter I wrote him. He had asked me to reconsider.

I sat in the diner and felt pain in my heart as I recalled that conversation. It flashed in my mind. Daniel had been sad about it, and I felt a wave of nausea as I remembered how insensitive I must have been.

I was in my own world, trying to be the free spirit Albert wanted. He was my Jim Morrison—the crazy, bad boy who I couldn't quite tame.

When I first met Albert, he had a squirrel for a pet, and I couldn't help but notice the similarities between Albert and that squirrel—attractive but unpredictable.

He was a hippie, plain and simple—free love and lots of drugs. I had been caught up in something that seemed attractive and worldly at the time, but now seemed regrettable.

I should have been a better friend to Daniel.

I should have been there for him.

I should have asked him how he felt and how he was doing in those letters, and instead, I just told him about my life and my boyfriends.

I experienced a rush of emotion, regret mostly. I was embarrassed. I felt my cheeks flame hot when I thought about some of the things we said in those letters.

I tried to remember if Daniel was in love with me. I didn't think he was at the time, but I would need to look at the letters again to be sure.

Maybe he had been.

My heart ached as I tried to recall.

"Ms. Nancy's coming," Tess said. She spoke discreetly and smiled as she glanced behind me. I could tell by her tone and expression that she was making eye contact with Nancy King. I could also tell by the way her line of vision changed that Nancy was getting closer to our table.

I turned to face Daniel's mom just as she walked up. Tess half-stood so she could give Nancy a one-armed hug. I did the same thing after my sister took a turn.

"Hey, Ms. Nancy," I said.

"Hey y'all. I'll sit for a second, just to get out of Betty's way." Nancy pulled back a chair and sat down in it. "I won't stay and interrupt your lunch, I just wanted to apologize for not making it to the shower last Saturday."

"Oh, goodness, that's okay," Tess said. "Billy said you were in Georgia with Daniel. We opened the gift you sent. Thank you so much! It's gorgeous. Right now, it's hard to imagine the baby being old enough to need a high chair, but that phase will be here before we know it."

Mrs. King shook her head. "Honey, you have no idea. You'll be putting a baby in that chair before you can count to ten.

When you do, remember this conversation. It'll amaze you how fast it gets here."

"I know, I'm kind of already seeing that," Tess said. She touched her belly. "It seems like yesterday I was telling Billy we were expecting, and now this."

"Yeah, and the next thing you know, he'll be a grown man, doing all sorts of things you never dreamed he would do."

"Yes, wow, Ms. Nancy. I meant to tell you congratulations," Tess said. "Abigail and I were just talking about Daniel. Please tell him congratulations for us."

Nancy smiled at my sister and then she glanced at me, holding the smile. "I'll tell him," she said with a nod. "It was amazing, seeing him there. It's the highest honor the military gives, and they made a big deal of it. They told his story, and had a whole presentation and everything."

"Oh, that's wonderful," Tess said.

Nancy nodded. "Nathaniel and I were so happy."

(They spoke quickly, talking over each other almost.)

"You must be so proud."

"We are."

"I bet. Wow."

"So thankful he's safe, too. Back at home."

"In Galveston?" Tess asked, looking surprised. "Billy said he thought he'd be another year or two."

"He will," Nancy said. "But he's back from overseas. That's what I meant. He's done serving, and he came back to the

States, but the Army loves him. They begged him to stay on. He's stationed over there at Fort Benning. He's training new recruits. His daddy wants him to take over the store eventually, but he's still young. He signed on for another year with the Army—but at least he'll be closer now. He loves it over in Georgia. I told his dad, I don't know if we'll ever get him home once he starts teaching over there."

"Oh, I'm surprised to hear that," Tess said. "Billy said he was planning on just doing a year or two and then for sure coming home."

"We'll see," Nancy said with a shrug. "I know he misses us and everything. But they treat him really good in the Army. They were already talking about trying to keep him on longer."

She stopped talking when Betty came to the table with our orders.

CHAPTER 2

"Sit with us!" Tess insisted. "I hardly ever get to catch up with you and Mister Nathaniel anymore. I miss you guys."

Nancy shifted and peered toward the kitchen. "I'm picking up a few hamburgers for the delivery crew," she said. "I suppose I can sit for just a minute, until my order's ready." She sighed and smiled as she turned to look at me. "So, what are you doing, Miss Abigail? Did you move back to town?"

She was being friendly, but with the way I was overanalyzing my shortcomings with Daniel, I automatically felt defensive and started over-thinking everything she did and said.

"No ma'am, I'm still back home in Louisiana. I was just here for the shower. I thought I would be here for the baby being born, too, but..." I hesitated comically, and Nancy chuckled accordingly.

"Are you past your due date now?" she asked, inspecting Tess, who nodded.

"Four days."

"Oh, how exciting! Any minute now. I wondered. I thought I would have heard something if you had it."

"No ma'am. Still waiting."

"You'll have to let us know when it happens so we can come by and meet the baby."

"I will," Tess said.

"Do you have a feeling about what it'll be?"

"Billy thinks it's gonna be a girl, but I don't know. I don't have a feeling either way."

"Billy wants a girl, huh? That's sweet. And you don't even have a guess?"

"No ma'am. And he'd be happy either way. I think he and Coach Marvin were taking bets up there at the gym—whether it's a girl or boy and how much it'll weigh."

"How funny," she said. "I think Nathaniel mentioned that. He might have gotten-in on it." Her eyes traveled toward the kitchen and she smiled and nodded at someone who was over there. "Well, look, ladies, I see our boxes at the bar. I'll let you go so you can eat your lunch. It was good seeing you both. Abigail, have a safe trip back home, sweetheart."

"Thank you," I said even though I couldn't shake the feeling that she didn't like me.

"And thank you and Mister Nathaniel for the high chair," Tess said. "We really do love it. Billy and I talked about what a handsome piece of furniture it is."

"You're welcome. We were happy to do that for you and Billy. We have several of Donnie's pieces. We like to support him, and it's a piece of furniture you can pass down to your children."

"I know, it's beautiful. Thank you. We'll take good care of it."

Nancy smiled. "Congratulations, sweetheart, and let us know when the baby comes."

"We will," Tess insisted nodding.

Nancy waved at both of us as she returned to the front of the restaurant where she would pick up her food and leave.

"Do you think she was upset with me? Is that why she was being short?" I asked.

"What do you mean *short*?" Tess asked, looking genuinely confused. She took a bite of her lunch.

"Don't you think it seemed like she was in a hurry?"

"No, not really," Tess said, shaking her head and chewing her food.

I thought about it as I took a bite of my sandwich. "I wonder if she's mad at me from when I stopped talking to Daniel," I said.

"I didn't think she was mad at you at all," Tess said, still looking confused.

I shrugged and smiled like she was probably right, but I didn't feel casual about it in my heart. I turned to look over my shoulder and saw Nancy paying for her food. I tried to figure out why seeing her made me feel bad. I was melancholy as a result of all these thoughts of Daniel and her visit to our table only made it worse. Nothing had been said to make me feel that way. Nancy was being friendly.

I was nostalgic for my friendship with Daniel, though, and suddenly filled with regret over ending it. I felt sick with myself about doing it at a time when he needed me the most.

"What happened, Abigail? What's the matter?" Tess asked the questions as if she was really concerned about me, and I realized my expression must have been reflecting my anxious thoughts.

"I was just thinking back," I said. "I was thinking about Daniel."

"What about him?"

"Those letters," I said dazedly. "I was remembering them, trying to. At the time, I was just…" I trailed off, feeling guilty for my selfishness. "I was preoccupied with my own stuff. I knew he was over there and everything, but I had feelings for…" I paused and took a bite of my sandwich for no other reason than to keep myself from crying. There was really no reason for me to be so worked up. I tried to tell myself that, but my emotions couldn't be controlled at the moment.

"For who?" Tess said, still looking confused.

"Albert," I said, pulling myself together, concentrating on my food. "I had feelings for Albert and everything, and I, I just feel bad. I'm just now realizing that Daniel probably thought we were… maybe he had some… feelings…" I sighed. "He probably thought things were different between us than I did.

I don't know. I need to get home and look at those letters again. I need to read them again."

"Don't beat yourself up," she said. "Things turned out okay for him. He did well."

"I know, and I'm glad. I'm just thinking that I probably wasn't a very good friend."

"Well, you could always call and tell him that," she said. "I'm sure it's fine though. I didn't even realize you guys were talking all that time. He talks to Billy quite a bit. It seems like he would've said something if he was upset with you or anything."

"Yeah," I agreed even though I took no comfort in the fact that he hadn't mentioned me to Billy.

I sat there and ate that sandwich and responded to Tess and the conversation she made, but I was preoccupied thinking about Daniel and remembering the sequence of events in our friendship. My thoughts were unorganized and interrupted, but during the course of that meal, I somehow reasoned with myself and concluded that Daniel had been in love with me the whole time—maybe even since the very beginning. I had never known it or accepted it. I had treated him so casually.

I ate most of my sandwich, but it was only to make myself seem normal. I was sick to my stomach.

"I'd like to go down to the boardwalk," I said to Tess on our way out.

"Really? Just to walk around?"

"Yeah," I said, nodding.

"Do you want to go alone?" she asked, looking at me as if gaging my mood.

"Not necessarily," I said. "A walk might do you good." I gestured to her stomach. "It might shake things up in there."

"I was thinking that same thing," Tess said, smiling.

The two of us went to the boardwalk.

I had been there lots of times. More recently, I went with Albert. But the memories that came to me as Tess and I walked were long ago memories—the ones that included Daniel King. I tried to force myself into not thinking of him. I tried to tell myself that I was only yearning for him because he got that big honor. I told myself that I regretted losing him now that he was some famous war hero.

But that wasn't what my heart felt.

I felt regret, but it wasn't the selfish type. I knew I wasn't good enough for Daniel now. I might have been at one point, but I hadn't seen it then. Now I had done things and made decisions that made me unworthy of someone like him.

I wasn't sad out of selfish regret. I truly did just want to make things right with him. But, then again, maybe that was selfish of me. Maybe I should just let him lead his life and not have the gratification of his forgiveness.

I went through the afternoon with my sister, saying the things she'd expect me to say so that she didn't know I was having a hard time internally. My regrets over Daniel were *my* problem, and I didn't want to put that on her—especially when she was about to give birth.

I left Galveston that evening, making Tess promise to call me as soon as they headed to the hospital.

I cried on my way home. I laughed, too. I was just emotional. I wasn't normally a dramatic type of person, but I was sad that I didn't get to meet the baby, and I was delirious with thoughts and memories regarding my relationship with Daniel King.

Regret, I decided, was the worst of all emotions. I was sad and embarrassed and full of regret, and I had no one to blame but myself.

I thought of how aloof I was at a time when Daniel was probably scared and definitely risking his life, and I felt sick with regret over it. That feeling only intensified when I got home to Starks and found the letters Daniel had written me.

I was currently living in an apartment with a roommate. It was a small complex owned by a friend of our family. I had been independent in college and then for a year in Galveston, so I was reluctant to move back in with my parents when I came home. I had been renting this apartment for a year. I carried a few things with me through all of my moves, and one of them was a box of letters. I had a few other keepsakes in there, but most of them were letters and most of those were from Daniel.

I went to the box the instant I got home. It had been a long time since I opened it, and I got a nostalgic feeling just from looking inside. I had gotten into the habit of putting the newest letters on top, so I simply sat the letters up on their side and started at the back of the pile, at the beginning. I read letters into the middle of the night. I stopped or took breaks, but all night, I kept going back to the box.

It was embarrassing how much I learned about Daniel. He wrote about things that I didn't even remember reading. Some of those letters, I wondered if I had even read them at all. One of them, I knew I hadn't read because it was literally still sealed. I cried when I opened it and during the whole time I read it. I didn't cry because it was sad, but more because Daniel assumed I already read the things he wrote.

It was two pages long, and he wrote about his training, his friends, and a few of his experiences that week. He had taken the time to write it, trusting that I would read it, and I had let him down. Even the ones that I knew I had read seemed foreign to me. I was able to see how much he liked me when I had been completely blind to it before.

I thought he was only my friend, but it was only because I wanted to see him that way. He hadn't felt that way about me at all. Daniel didn't pour his heart out in the letters, but he made it known that he carried a torch for me. I didn't have my letters to him, obviously, but I knew I had been casual. I cared for Daniel, but he was two years younger than me, and I had just seen him as a friend.

I thought back to what he looked like when we had first met. He had a busted nose on day one that had been given to him by Billy. This was before they became friends and before Billy married my sister.

I had a history with Daniel, and I was ashamed of myself for just letting it end so casually.

I had to reach out and let him know that I was sorry about that. I decided I would find him and apologize. It couldn't be that hard. I knew he was in Fort Benning, Georgia. If all else failed, I could contact his parents and they could tell me how to reach him.

CHAPTER 3

My phone rang the following afternoon.

I fully expected to hear Daniel's voice when I answered it. My body experienced a jolt of excitement. I had spent the better part of my morning trying to locate Daniel on a huge Army base and getting his current phone number. I had left a message for him telling him I would be home any time after 1pm. It was just after two, and I was excited that he had called back so soon.

I had been listening for the phone, so I picked up after the first ring. "Hello?" I said, trying to hide the fact that I had run to the phone and was now out of breath.

"Abigail Cohen," Daniel said. "How are you?" His voice was deep and patient, and I ached a little at the sound of it.

"Daniel King," I said, answering him. We were both smiling. It was obvious by how we sounded, and it was a gigantic relief on my end. "I'm good," I said. "Everything's good. I'm about to start teaching. It's my second year. I had a meeting this morning. What about you?" I stopped talking to catch my breath.

"I'm good too," he said.

"I heard."

"You heard about what?" he asked.

"Your medal. My goodness. I saw your mom, and she was telling us about that medal you got. Congratulations, Daniel, what an honor. I knew you could do something great."

"Thank you," he said. "That was an honor. I was glad they could be here for it."

I was breathless, but Daniel didn't seem nervous at all. In fact, he was so patient and mellow that I thought he might be indifferent about hearing from me. Maybe it was just that I was so nervous. I had about a million things to say to Daniel, but suddenly, I couldn't think of any of them.

"I ran into your mom yesterday," I said, grasping at straws.

"Yeah, that's what you were saying on the message you left earlier," he said.

"I saw her at Carson's, but only for a minute."

"So, you're still living in Galveston?" he asked.

My heart pounded at the sound of his voice. It was familiar— maybe more confident than it used to be, but familiar. I had no idea why I was so wrecked.

"No, no, I'm in Starks. I'm back home in Louisiana. I got a job teaching at the elementary school. I'm just about to start my second year."

"Oh, okay. That's great. What grade?"

"First," I said. I was still catching my breath and trying not to sound like it.

"Oh, well that's good. That's what you wanted," he said.

"Yeah. Your mom said you were done with being overseas but that you were planning on staying in Georgia for another year."

"Yeah, I signed-on for another year, but I won't go overseas again. I'll stay here. I might sign another contract after this trial year is up, but I'm not sure. I'll have to see how I like teaching and... living in Georgia."

"Doesn't your dad want you to come back and take over the store?"

"Eventually. But he's not trying to retire right now. I have a few years before I have to think about that."

"I was going to tell you that, Daniel, you know, if you're s-staying away, I just, I wanted to say, you know, that'd I'd love to write to you again. I was thinking about it so much, and going through some of the old letters, and... I'm sorry I failed you a couple of years ago. I made a huge mistake by telling you to stop writing me. I'm so sorry. If you'd be willing to let me, I could write twice a week like we said at first—or once—whatever you would want to do. I promise I wouldn't miss this time. I'll write certain days of the week like you did. I'm really sorry for the time I wasn't there for you, and I'd love to make it right. I'd love to talk again and catch up."

I was so nervous that my ramblings were breathless and quiet. I paused, and Daniel went so long without responding that I thought he had been cut off or that maybe he hadn't heard me. Maybe it would be a good thing if he hadn't.

"Hello?" I said.

"I'm here," he said.

"Oh, did you hear me?"

"Yes. I just… you really don't have to feel bad," he said.

"I can't help it," I said. "I do feel bad. I was a bad friend to you. I shouldn't have told you to stop writing me. I'm sorry."

"It's okay," Daniel said.

"No, it's not. I'm sorry. I would love to write to you again. If you want. I know I'm late, and you're not overseas anymore, but…"

"Well, I'm sort of in the same situation you were in the last time we talked," Daniel said.

"What? What do you mean?"

Daniel was quiet for a few seconds. "I mean, I'm in the same situation as you were in back then. I think if I would start writing you, maybe Kelly, the girl I'm seeing now, would get hurt by that."

"Oh, you're, Kelly? You're seeing a girl named… Kel… you're… yeah… oh, yeah, definitely. I didn't know you were… I wasn't trying to say that… I was just, you know, talking about writing as friends or whatever. Wanting to catch up."

I clamped my mouth shut. I literally covered my mouth with my own hand. My heart pounded. I closed my eyes. My own blood pumping was causing my ears to ring.

"I'm sorry," Daniel said. "It's really new, this thing between Kelly and me. She's from here, actually. I only met her a couple of weeks ago."

"Oh, no, I totally... I wasn't saying it like that, anyway. But I totally understand about not wanting to be in touch with me at all if you're with someone."

"Well, it's new, like I said. I introduced her as a friend to my parents when they came, but you know, it's been a few weeks, and I would hate to..." He trailed off briefly, but it was long enough that I started babbling again.

"Oh, yeah, definitely. That's great. That's exciting for you— that you met someone. I'm glad your parents got to meet her, too. I saw your mom, but she didn't mention..." I was going to say she didn't mention meeting a woman, but I just gave up and stopped talking in the middle of a sentence.

There were a few seconds of awkward silence.

"I hadn't heard from you in so long that I just assumed we probably wouldn't talk again," he said.

"Yeah, oh, yeah. No, yeah. I figured that, too. I just saw your mom, and I... I'm... I was... I don't even live in Galveston. I did—for a year, you know, but not anymore. I'm back home in Louisiana now." I took a slow, deep breath, trying my best to compose myself. "I was just thinking about old times after I saw your mom. Tess is about to have her baby, so I was in Galveston for the shower and everything. I just came back home yesterday. She still hasn't had the baby."

"Yeah, I talked to Billy yesterday."

"Oh, really? Billy? Yesterday?"

"We talk every other week or so," Daniel said. "I thought I would have heard about the baby by now, so I called him yesterday."

"Oh, I didn't know you and Billy still talked that much."

I hadn't talked to Daniel in two years. I had talked to Billy a lot in that time, but he never mentioned Daniel or told me that they kept in contact. I felt embarrassed, humiliated, rejected, overflowing with guilt and regret.

"I'm so sorry, Daniel."

"Don't be sorry, Abby. I'm happy to hear from you." His voice was deep and genuine, full of care and concern, full of forgiveness.

"I know. I'm happy to hear from you, too," I said even though I hadn't technically heard from him.

In that moment, I realized that I had my heart set on trying to be with Daniel when I called him. I thought I just wanted to make amends with him, to make things right from when I abandoned him, but that wasn't the truth. I also wanted him to like me. I wanted to pick up where we left off. I knew this because my heart felt broken when he told me he was with someone else.

I had to get past that.

I had to think of him and not me.

I knew I had to act fast before I lost the nerve.

"I know you're seeing someone," I said. "And I don't want to keep you too long or get you in trouble with that or anything, but I just wanted to talk to you for a minute. I don't know how to say this other than to say 'thank you'. Thanks for everything you did over there, Daniel. I was talking to my dad about it this morning, and he said that you had to do something really brave to have gotten that medal, and I just wanted to… I don't know… say thanks for doing that. And to tell you I'm proud of you for going over there and being so brave and everything… and that I'm sorry that I… wasn't there for you more." I got choked up while I was speaking, and I had to pause and speak slowly to get the words out, but I did it. My speech wasn't graceful sounding, but I managed, and I said the things that had been on my heart.

There were a few seconds of silence where I just waited, heart pounding, for Daniel to say something.

"Thank you," he said, finally. "Thank you for saying that, Abby."

He was so sincere and thoughtful that I couldn't help but let out a sigh. "Please don't," I said. "I don't feel like I deserve to be thanked." Hot stinging tears rose to my eyes, and I was glad we were on the phone so Daniel couldn't see me cry. I didn't even worry about wiping my face, I just let the tears fall onto my cheeks since I was alone in the room. "I'm calling to thank *you*," I said, speaking softly and controlling my voice through the silent tears. "And to ask your forgiveness. I didn't realize how selfish I was being. I'm sorry for telling you not to write me. I shouldn't have done that." I sighed.

"You don't have to apologize," Daniel said.

He was being a gentleman, but I needed him to hear my sorrow and regret. "I know. I knew you would say something like that, but this is one of those times where I did wrong and I need to apologize for it."

"Okay," he said. "I can respect that."

A few seconds of silence passed.

"I should have treated you better," I said. "I took our friendship for granted, and I'm sorry about it. I should have done better."

"Thank you," he said.

"I'm really happy to hear you're happy, though. And that you made it through everything all right. Did you have to go through some hard stuff over there, in Vietnam?"

"Yes, I did," he said. He spoke with such calm certainty that I knew he was telling the truth.

"Anything you want to talk about?" I asked.

"Uh… huh?"

"Is there anything you would want to tell me? Anything you'd like to get off your chest from over there? Or anywhere?"

"Uhhh." Daniel made a hesitant noise, and then cut off with a chuckle. I could hear him hesitating. "No, I don't guess," he said. "They have special people for me to talk to about that stuff."

"Why, because it's top secret?"

"No, because it's not anything you'd want to hear."

"Try me," I said.

"Abby, let's just put it this way. I saw stuff I will never talk about again. Not even to those people who are trained to ask me about it. Certain details of battle, I'm just gonna keep to myself. As far as catching you up on me and what I'm doing, I'm good. I had something happen to my right leg, and at first they told me I wouldn't walk again, but I've been real persistent with healing it, and it's doing good. I barely have a limp now. Most people don't even notice. I'm able to jog on it and everything."

"Your mom didn't say anything about you getting hurt."

"She knew I was hurt, but she doesn't know the extent of it. I didn't tell her most of the stuff I went through. There was no sense in her worrying."

I felt a pain in my heart. I should've been there for him. I should've been the person he could tell about things he went through. I didn't say anything else, though. I had already apologized, and I didn't want to keep harping on it.

"Did you have to fight in actual battles?"

"Yes."

"Were you scared?"

"Yes, I was," he said with a little chuckle.

"Were there times you thought you wouldn't come home?" I asked.

"Yes, there were those times." He was answering in short answers, but he was speaking slowly, like he wasn't in a hurry to get off the phone.

Daniel and I talked for two hours that afternoon.

We asked each other questions and took turns answering them. We answered honestly, but we kept the conversation light. He told me some of his non-battle experiences of being in the military, and I told him some about my life as a teacher.

I didn't ask him about the girl he was dating. I respected that he was talking to someone else, and I didn't flirt with him or anything, but I also didn't bring her up or encourage their relationship in any way.

We talked for so long that by the end of it, I felt a lot better. Daniel was a gentleman—a kind, considerate, funny, well-rounded man. I had taken him for granted, I had made a huge mistake, but at least he had turned out great. I would have felt a lot worse if I had done what I did and he wound up having all sorts of troubles. I did feel better after talking to him.

CHAPTER 4

Three months later
Thanksgiving
Galveston Island, TX

*F*or the last few years, Tess and Billy had been hosting Thanksgiving at their house in Galveston. Our mom always wanted us to be in Starks for Christmas, but Thanksgiving was the holiday that Tess and Billy could share with some of their close friends in Galveston. Marvin Jones was one of them. He was a famous boxer from the forties and also Billy's head coach, mentor, and friend. There were always others from the gym, too. It had become a tradition in the last couple of years, and now we all just assumed we were having Thanksgiving with Billy and Tess.

I had the entire week off school, so I went a day early to help Tess plan, buy groceries, and prepare the dishes. Everything took longer nowadays since she had a three-month-old baby.

Billy had been right. She gave birth to a daughter—a beautiful black-haired girl named Tara Grace. I called her Tara-bo-bara and things like that. She was the most precious thing ever, and Billy and Tess were in love.

Counting family, we were expecting to feed thirteen to fifteen people. Matty and Tony, two of Billy's friends from way back, said they'd just be stopping by. But we knew from experience that they wouldn't turn down a plate of food. Quentin from the gym was coming, and he might or might not be bringing his girlfriend and her sister.

All these extra guests were fine by us because Tess, our mother, and I all loved Thanksgiving. We loved cooking the traditional Thanksgiving meal with turkey, ham, veggies, and casseroles. We enjoyed serving a holiday feast, and Tess and Billy's friends always seemed eager to eat with us.

Our mother would start cooking her share of the meal back home in Louisiana before dawn on Thursday. Then she'd transport the hot dishes to Galveston Thursday morning. Tess and I would take care of everything else except the rolls, which Marvin would make from scratch and bring over when he came.

We planned on eating a late lunch so that everyone had enough time to arrive and get nice and hungry. I loved Thanksgiving, and I had been looking forward to this meal and this fellowship for months. It was almost 1pm, and most of the guests had already arrived. We were missing Dizzy and his wife, but they were on their way. We were also missing Matty and Tony, but we didn't expect them to be there before we got started.

I was dressed festively for the occasion. In general, I wore a lot of skirts and dresses. I wore pants, too, but I liked how skirts looked on me and I felt comfortable in them. I had on a denim skirt with red tights and a striped sweater. I was wearing the colors of fall, and I was in good spirits.

I was feeling that way right up until 1pm on the dot when Billy came up to us in the kitchen and said, "Daniel's here."

Panic.

Instant panic.

"Daniel King?" I asked, my head whipping around to face Billy when he said it. "Daniel King?" I repeated when he didn't answer right away.

I would have never dreamed Billy would say that. I didn't even know Daniel was in Galveston. I stared at Billy who was now nodding in answer to my question.

"I wasn't going to say anything," Billy said. "I invited him last week, and he said he'd come. I was just gonna let him come in and surprise everybody. But he called a few minutes ago to see if we needed anything, and he told me he's got his lady friend with him."

"He's bringing a date?" Tess asked.

I glanced at her to find that she was looking at Billy with wide eyes. She blinked.

Billy nodded. "His friend from Georgia. Kelly. I figured we had plenty for one more. I mean, it's not like we'll run out of food."

"I know we won't run out of food, but…" Tess trailed off and looked at me, asking me without saying a word if I was okay. Billy had other things to do, so he wasn't paying attention to our facial expressions. Marvin was across the room, in the middle of telling a story, and he was yelling over to Billy for confirmation on something.

I was stirring the gravy. It was the final thing I was working on, and I needed to concentrate to get it right.

But how was I supposed to concentrate?

How could Daniel bring a woman over here?

What was I supposed to do?

Should I stay?

Could I stay?

I wasn't even sure if I could muster up the will to stay and sit through lunch with him sitting next to another girl.

Of course I would stay.

There was no other choice but to stay.

I had been in a good mood all morning, and it would be weird and completely obvious if I up-and-left right after Billy gave me that bit of information about Daniel. I knew I had to stay, and at the same time, I just didn't know if I could. I felt compelled to leave before they got there. I wanted to be gone and not have to see either of them.

Why would he do that?

Why would he come here with another girl?

Why did I care?

I had no right to care. I stirred the gravy non-stop, my thoughts swimming as I stared at the swirling liquid. A few minutes ago, I was starving, and now I didn't feel like eating at all.

I had to get out of there. I would make up an excuse and leave. I had a good friend named Evelyn who was spending Thanksgiving with her family. I usually went by there later in the afternoon. I would simply bump up my plans and go now. I knew I'd be welcome at her house.

"I might leave," I said, turning to speak directly to my sister who was standing beside me.

She had just taken the ham out of the oven and was in the process of taking off her oven mitts. Our mom was standing across the way holding the baby. Dad was looking over her shoulder. People were having conversations. No one was paying attention to me. No one would really even notice if I slipped out.

"Why?" Tess asked. "Because of Daniel? Did you try talking to him?"

"Yes," I whispered. "And I'm too nervous to stay."

"No, you're not," Tess said. "It's just Daniel."

"Yeah," I said, nodding casually even though I didn't feel casual at all. Tess didn't know how much I had been thinking about him, and I didn't plan on telling her. She knew I had talked to Daniel a few months ago when I apologized, but she had no idea how much he had been on my mind or that I was still plagued by regret. No one did.

I hadn't seen him in so long that I had no idea what to expect. He could have scars or a beard and I would know nothing of it. It was possible that I wouldn't recognize him at all. I pictured him walking in with his Army uniform on.

"I think it's ready," Tess said, leaning in front of me to turn off the stove. I glanced at her to find that she was looking at my gravy.

My head was swimming.

I was normally a rational, resilient human being. I had no idea why I was reacting like this. I was out-of-my-mind with anticipation for his arrival.

"Listen, I'm going to stay as long as I can, but if I sneak out, just please don't make a big deal about it."

"Why would you sneak out, Abigail? Where would you go?"

"Evelyn's. Her parents have a lot of people over every year."

Tess already knew that, so she nodded, but she was looking at me like she didn't quite understand. "Are you mad that Daniel's bringing his girlfriend?"

"I'm not mad, I'm just… I don't know what I'm going to feel. I don't know what to expect. I haven't seen him in a long time."

And within seconds, I heard him come in the door. Just as that was happening, Billy made the announcement that everyone needed to gather in the kitchen, so things got louder and louder as ten or twelve people made their way in there with us. Tess and Billy had a large, two-story Victorian home, but it felt a lot smaller with all those people now standing in the kitchen with us.

I knew Daniel had come in. I hadn't seen him yet, but I could tell he was there by how the energy in the room shifted. I could hear people talking to him and saying his name. I even glanced at the area near the door and saw the edge of his arm, but I couldn't bear to look at him.

There were enough people in the room that I didn't have to make a spectacle just to remain unseen. Our parents had gotten closer to me with all the shifting, and I easily hid behind my father, putting him between Daniel and myself when everyone moved into the room. I looked again and caught a glimpse of his side, just enough to notice that he wasn't wearing an army uniform. It looked like he had on jeans and a t-shirt.

I couldn't help but notice the blonde standing next to him. She was Barbie-doll blonde, Marilyn Monroe blonde. I could not bring myself to look at either of them.

Fine. I looked at her. Just a glance. Oh, gosh. She was really pretty. Of course she was.

I hated her instantly. I already had bad thoughts about her before today. I had decided that she stalked Fort Benning, waiting for the perfect man to go through there, and when he did, she dug her claws into him. Seeing her only made it worse. I knew all my worst fears were true. She made herself into a perfect girl so she could stalk and trap the perfect Army guy.

I glanced at her again, and she was smiling brightly and talking to Dizzy, who was standing near her. She was probably the nicest person in the world, but it was easier for me to make all this up about her having devious plans.

I didn't like her. I couldn't help it. I wasn't going to treat her badly, but I had no desire to talk to her. I hated her for being smarter than me, which was probably a weird sort of compliment, or at least a form of respect.

I had these sorts of thoughts while Billy and my sister said a few things about Thanksgiving and how happy they were to have everyone at their house.

They introduced Tara. I looked straight at the baby, smiling and trying to seem normal even though I was out-of-my-head with emotions. Moments ago, I had been stirring gravy casually while in a great mood, and now I was stiff and cripplingly distracted with my blood rushing and thoughts ripping through my mind.

I absentmindedly listened to Billy and Tess. Their speech ended with announcing that everyone could get in line to serve themselves in the kitchen before taking plates to the dining room, living room, or wherever they could find a spot.

We had an amazing lineup of food, and as soon as Tess stopped talking, everyone began murmuring about how good everything looked and smelled as they shifted to get in line.

There were two ways in and out of the kitchen, thank goodness. I took off my apron, stashed it on a nearby countertop before slipping out of the kitchen using the exit that was nowhere near Daniel. I went toward the dining room. I would have to walk through it to get to the hallway, but that was no problem.

Quentin's girlfriend and her sister were in the dining room, and I smiled at them and mumbled something about going to use the restroom. But they didn't care, they just smiled at me and headed to the kitchen.

I felt ridiculously bad—terrible. I hadn't stared at Daniel, but I had seen enough to realize that he had grown up. He was tall and broad-chested, and he had some facial hair. It was the man version of the old Daniel King, and seeing him was difficult for me.

I walked through the dining room and down the hallway. There was a bathroom in the hall, but I kept going, through Tess and Billy's bedroom and into their master bathroom. This way, I wouldn't be disturbed.

I knew I had no right to make this about me, but at the same time, I just couldn't control the feelings I was having. Physically, I felt the need to run. I just couldn't be there. I made a plan as I walked into the bathroom. I would go in there for a minute to gather my thoughts, but I had to leave pretty quickly and sneak through the living room while everyone else was still in the kitchen and dining room. I had said enough to my sister that she would know where and why I had gone. I would need to try to get to my mother to let her know what was going on. I would see if I could do that on my way out.

I went through the motions of using the restroom, washing my hands, and checking myself in the mirror. Doing things like that helped me keep from thinking about other things too much, which kept me from crying.

Daniel had always been handsome, but now he was a man—a real man. His face had filled out and was now chiseled and masculine. I had been mad at myself for three months over this, and being faced with him in person was simply overwhelming.

I took a brief moment in the bathroom, and then I headed through Tess and Billy's bedroom to go back to the party. I would find my mom, let her know where I was going, and then make my way out. I was concentrating on leaving with as little drama as possible. I had my head down and I was focused on finding my mother.

I walked through their bedroom quickly and turned the corner to head down the hall.

I ran into him instantly.

I didn't just encounter Daniel in the hallway, I literally ran straight into him, bumping up against him before pulling back clumsily.

"Oh, hey," I said.

"Hey! Come here, Abby-girl. I haven't seen you in forever. Give me a hug."

CHAPTER 5

A hug?
A hug?

Was he asking me for a hug?

Was Daniel King standing, big as an ox, in my sister's hallway with his arms casually outstretched in front of me? How was he asking me for a hug when his beautiful girlfriend was waiting for him in the next room?

I smiled stiffly, leaned in, and awkwardly hugged him, letting my head barely touch his chest while tapping his big back with my fingertips.

I hardly recognized him.

He was a strapping young man. His chest and arms seemed like they had doubled in size since the last time I saw him. He was bigger than his dad. He wrapped his arms around me and gave me a tight but quick squeeze.

We broke apart, and I looked at him to find that he was smiling at me as a big brother would. I had been confident in my fall outfit, but now that I was looking at Daniel, I felt plain.

He was gorgeous—the most handsome man I had ever seen. His hair had darkened. Or maybe that was his beard. He didn't have facial hair before.

"You have a beard now," I said feeling the need to say something after the awkward hug. I could hardly breathe.

Daniel smiled and touched his face. "Barely," he said. "I had a week off, so I let it grow out. I have to be clean-shaven for work, so I'll have to get rid of it next week."

I smiled at him. I was looking at his face but honestly trying not to take it in.

"I didn't know you were coming," I said.

"The trip was sort of last minute."

We could hear voices, but they were off in the distance. We were alone in the hallway, standing only a few feet apart. I stepped back, leaning against the doorway of the bedroom. Daniel was so perfect that my heart ached from looking at him.

"I was actually going to eat at Evelyn's," I said. "I was here to help Tess get ready and everything, but I sort of had plans to… Evelyn's parents have a big lunch every year with her family and everything, and they invited me."

"Oh, you're leaving?" he asked, looking confused.

"Yeah, I was going to slip out," I said. "I was just helping Tess get everything ready."

"Why would you leave?" he asked. "I was excited to see you—excited to catch up. Can't you just stay for lunch?"

I started to say something but then I hesitated with my mouth open. "I—uh, I, need to… I told Evelyn that I would… I didn't want to…" I spoke slowly as I gazed at him. I realized I was staring, but there was nothing I could do to stop myself.

"You didn't want to, what?" he asked.

"Huh?"

"You were telling me why you were leaving. You said you didn't want to do something."

"I didn't want to… see… you…" I said the words in a dazed sort of state where I could think of nothing besides the truth.

"Me?" Daniel said, sounding genuinely surprised. "You don't want to see me?"

"I do, I do. I really do," I said quietly, smiling and fumbling for words. "I just meant that I feel a little… overwhelmed about it." I paused for a second or two, taking him in and trying to figure out what I was feeling.

"Why are you overwhelmed?" he asked, tilting his head at me.

I tried to step around him, and he put his hand out to stop me. It was what I wanted him to do. I wanted him to stop me. And yet I didn't know what to say now that he had.

"Daniel, I… the main thing I want is for you to be happy." I cut my eyes toward the kitchen. "I know you're happy and your girlfriend is probably great and everything, and that's what I want. I'm glad. That makes me happy." I paused, blinking at him, staring into his hazel green eyes. "I just can't see it," I whispered. "I'm glad it exists, but I don't want to look at it. You can be happy something exists and still not be able to look at it. I hope that makes enough sense and you know it's nothing against you or anything. I really do... love... seeing you... Daniel." My words came out choppy sounding, which only added to the odd things I was saying. I was not expecting any of this and I was having trouble putting my thoughts into words.

Daniel was staring at me like he didn't quite understand. "Please don't go," he said. "Seeing you was one of the main reasons I came over here. It's been years, Abby."

"I know," I said, nodding.

He obviously didn't understand how affected I was at this moment, which made the whole thing hurt even more.

I knew I needed to toughen up. I owed it to Daniel to make this encounter as pleasant as possible for him. I nodded and took a deep breath.

"I can wait and go to Evelyn's a little later," I said with a smile.

"Thank you," he said. He put his hand on my shoulder. "I know you don't live in Galveston anymore, and I was hoping to catch up while you're here. I haven't seen you in so long."

I just stared up at him. I wanted to pour my heart out. I wanted to beg him to give me another chance. "Yeah, yeah, that'll be good," I said, trying to seem way less shaken than I was.

I had been blindsided by his arrival.

I really wished I had seen it coming.

I fully intended on leaving, but I couldn't now that I had run into Daniel and told him I would stay. I made my way from the hallway back to the kitchen.

I didn't even look to see if Daniel was following me. I didn't want to walk in there with him. I felt like my feelings were so obvious that I might as well have a sign on my forehead that said *I'm in love with Daniel King.*

I had to leave him in the hallway and go back into the kitchen alone.

I went straight to the baby. Tess was holding her while explaining to Marvin where he could find the extra napkins.

"I'll take her and change her diaper," I said, walking up to my sister.

"She actually does need it," Tess said, handing her to me. "Thank you. I'll feed her after that, and she'll probably take a nap."

I gingerly took the baby from her. There was so much going on in the kitchen that no one was paying attention to us. I vaguely noticed that Daniel came back into the kitchen and joined his girlfriend who was still standing on the other side. I avoided looking their way.

I took Tara to the nursery to change her.

I stayed back there with her for several minutes. I kept seeing Daniel in my mind's eye. The memory of him in the hallway was too much. I thought of his stature and how it had changed. I thought of what it felt like when he hugged me. He was no longer a boy. He was a man now, in form and in confidence. It made my stomach tie in knots when I remembered the sight of him a few minutes ago.

"Just tell me to forget all about that," I said to Tara, who stared at me from the crib where I was changing her diaper. "Tell me to get that out of my head." I glanced at her eyes, and she stared back, wiggling. I smiled and shook my head like she was saying something to me. "I know. I can't believe he brought her, either," I said. "She's not even pretty," I added, lying.

I fastened Tara's outfit and said a few things to her about other topics. I knew she didn't really understand me, but I didn't want our whole talk to be about Daniel. I told her she was beautiful and pumped her up to go back out to the party. She liked to look around, but her neck wasn't sturdy yet. I propped her up where she was cradled in my arm but could still look out, and I took off for the kitchen.

Daniel came into the nursery just as I made it to the door. I instantly looked behind him to see if he was alone. My eyes snapped up to meet his when I saw that he was.

"I had to come make sure you weren't leaving," he said. "You said you were going to stay, but then you took off."

"Oh, I was just... changing the baby."

Daniel stared down at little Tara, wearing a sweet smile. His nose wasn't completely straight. That injury had happened the first day I saw him. It was better than straight, though, honestly. I didn't know what it looked like before, but I couldn't imagine liking it more than I did right now. There was a small dent in the bridge, and somehow it made him look way better that way than if it was perfect.

He came close to us, staring at the baby. I imagined, for a second, that the moment was ours—that Daniel was mine and the baby was ours. It would have been a perfect moment if that were reality. But it wasn't reality, and that harsh truth fell on me like a piano out of the sky when Jayne Mansfield came into the doorway.

"Kelly, come see this baby," Daniel said, without skipping a beat.

She walked into the room, and my heart felt like it was being poured out of my chest. She smiled at me and then at Tara. "Is this your baby?" she asked.

"It's my sister's," I said. "I'm Aunt Abby."

"Aw, she's adorable," Kelly said, looking at Tara. "I think I'll use the restroom," she added, shifting to stare at Daniel.

"It's just right there in the hall," I said. "On the left."

"Do you live here?" she asked.

"Me? No. I've thought about it. I love Galveston, and Tess and Billy have extra bedrooms upstairs. But no. I live in Louisiana."

"Are all these people in your family?" she asked me.

"No, my mom and dad are here, but otherwise it's all Tess and Billy's friends. Tess is my sister."

"And Billy's the boxer," she said.

"He is," I said, nodding. "He's famous. Marvin is probably more famous. Marvin Jones. But Billy's really successful. He'll be remembered like Marvin one day."

"She knows Billy," Daniel said. "Her dad's a big boxing fan. We talk about Billy."

"My dad met Cassius Clay," she said. "Muhammed Ali."

"Wow, that's pretty cool," I said.

I had been in the same room with Muhammed Ali before with Tess and Billy. I didn't meet him, but I could've gone up to him if I were that type and it was important to me. Either way, I wasn't going to tell Kelly that. I let out a sigh because I didn't know what to say.

"Well, I guess we better go get some of that yummy food," I said. I realized that the phrase *yummy food* was just about the dorkiest thing I could say, and yet it still came out of my mouth. Yummy food. It sounded to me like I delivered it half-speed.

I smiled and nodded and took off toward the kitchen. I almost called some sort of closing statement over my shoulder to Kelly about how it was nice to meet her, but I didn't. I just walked down the hall, leaving them to use the restroom or whatever they were going to do.

I left that room thinking that my Thanksgiving was about to get a lot better. It had to. It couldn't possibly get any worse than being trapped in the back room with Daniel and his girlfriend as they recounted stories of her dad meeting famous boxers.

I would simply go in there, make a plate, and find a place to sit where there wasn't room for the two of them. I would smile and act normal and avoid them for the rest of the afternoon.

CHAPTER 6

I went through Thanksgiving lunch with a smile, talking to people like I normally would. But it was difficult. Guilt, shame, and regret were the worst of all emotions because they were things that got brought on by yourself.

I felt nothing but regret as I witnessed Daniel King interacting with everyone at lunch. It wasn't just that I ruined my own chances of being with him. It was mainly because I regretted being so aloof for so long when he obviously had feelings for me. The memory of it made me feel like a terrible person.

I wasn't mean to him. I was his friend, and we talked and laughed like friends do, but I completely ignored his affections, and he was worth so much more than that. I felt ashamed that he had gone through hard situations while I was being selfish and neglecting him.

But continuing to fret over it would only result in further wasted time. I decided that sometimes feeling too guilty about something could inadvertently morph into a selfish act.

I went through the afternoon in a good mood, trying my best to avoid looking at those two specific people without seeming like I was avoiding it.

It was easy. There were plenty of people to occupy me so that my behavior toward Daniel didn't seem questionable. I did overhear a conversation where he talked about his plans for the weekend. He said he wasn't going back to Georgia until Sunday.

I had two reactions to hearing that, neither of them felt particularly healthy.

For one, I was excited that he was staying. The instant I heard he would be here till Sunday I started changing my plans so that I could stay a day longer with Tess and Billy. This way, I at least had a *chance* of running into him again.

The second emotion I felt was jealousy. I thought of them traveling together. I thought of them spending nights together. I didn't think Daniel would get so close to someone so quickly, and it made me feel sick to my stomach.

***

I did end up staying with Tess and Billy through the weekend with plans to head back to Louisiana on Sunday, but I didn't push the idea of running into Daniel again. I could have tried to make it happen. I could have simply called him or gone to his house, but I didn't feel good about it.

That was a difficult moral dilemma for me. On one hand, I felt like I didn't deserve him and I should give up and not bother him or his newfound happiness. And on the other hand, that felt like I was giving up too quickly. Part of me thought, he's not married, and I should still pursue him or I would regret it forever, and the other part was convinced I shouldn't do it.

I told myself that I would love it if I ran into Daniel again that weekend by accident, but I wasn't going to force it. My best chance of it happening was going to be Saturday afternoon at the boxing gym.

Billy was a full-time professional athlete. He made his livelihood as a prizefighter. He loved what he did and he treated it like a full-time job. He was at the gym constantly. He would be there all day on Saturday, and at around 3pm, Tess and I would bring a batch of cold, fresh-cut fruit up there for everybody to enjoy. It was something she did once a week or so. It was all her idea.

I was excited about going, though, because Daniel's dad's hardware store was on the same block as Bank Street Boxing. The two were right across the street from each other. I had no reason to believe that Daniel would be at the hardware store while we were at the gym, but I still got butterflies in my stomach at the thought of it.

I ended up running into Daniel in spectacular fashion.

I thought maybe I'd bump into him (and the girl) on Bank Street on our way into the gym. But that wasn't at all what happened. It was one of those glorious moments in life where reality blew away my fantasies.

Daniel was *inside* the gym when we got there.

Music was playing, and it was crowded, so it took me a minute to spot him. He had on headgear and no shirt, and he was in the ring on the far side of the gym, sparring with Billy.

I knew who he was the instant I laid eyes on him.

I stared.

Somewhere in the back of my mind, I figured his girlfriend was there, too, but I didn't care enough to take my eyes off of him and search for her.

"We usually just set this out here on the table," Tess said, assuming I was wondering about the fruit, which I wasn't. My throat was closed, and I almost choked as I started to talk. I could not believe that a shirtless Daniel King was in the same room as me. I could not believe I was so affected by seeing him.

I had seen a lot of shirtless guys in my life. In my teenage years, I was a connoisseur of the male form. I very much enjoyed putting myself in positions like the beach or pools where I had views of shirtless guys. I had seen and inspected many a young man in my day. I had mellowed out about being boy-crazy now, but I still had good taste, and I was still able to appreciate the sight of a gorgeous human being.

Daniel King was flawless.

He was so much bigger, broader than he had been four years ago. He seemed like skin and bones back then by comparison. Now he was a man with full-size man muscles. I watched him as we walked around the ring. He was still Daniel, he was just so much smoother, more solid, more substantial. He was confident in his movements. I saw him smiling as he and Billy exchanged blows. They were light on their feet, working hard, but going at what seemed to be about half-strength.

I could see and take in all of this as we made our way to the table. Tess was holding the baby, and I was holding the huge bowl of fruit. She stopped in front of the table gesturing to it. She told me what to do, and I went through the motions of putting out the fruit, bowls, and the toothpicks.

"Get a bowl full for Billy and Daniel, please," she said. "Or hold Tara while I do it."

"I got it," I said. "One bowl each, or one bowl to share?"

"One each," she said. "Thank you." She took the baby and started walking toward the boxing ring at the back of the gym, leaving me there to scoop two portions of fruit salad into a bowl.

"What you got here, little Miss Abigail?"

I knew it was Marvin's voice before I even turned and saw him. "Watermelon, cantaloupe, grapes, and oranges," I said smiling at him. "We had it in the freezer for a little while before we came over here, so it's all really cold."

Marvin's hand touched my arm. "You might want to cover your ears," he said.

I reached up and did as he said, and he turned and let out a loud whistle. All of the people in the gym, ten or fifteen people, stopped what they were doing and turned to look at Marvin.

He cleared his throat. "The Castros, along with my friend, Abigail here, were nice enough to bring us a little refreshment. Y'all better come get some while it's cold. It just came out of the freezer."

No one hesitated. They all began flocking to the table. Fresh fruit was something they were used to—a few of them even stopped what they were doing and headed over before Marvin ever whistled.

"You got yourself some?" Marvin asked, stepping back to let the sweaty athletes access the table.

"No sir, these are for Daniel and Billy. Tess and I ate enough while we were cutting it. All the ends and side-pieces, we just kept popping them into our mouths."

Marvin laughed. I held up the bowls and gestured with a tilt of my head toward the back of the gym.

"I'm going to take these to the boys," I said. "Unless you want one," I added. I held one of the bowls toward him. "I could make another one for them if you want to take this one."

"No, thank you, Miss Abby. You go on ahead and take those to the boys. I'll get in here and get me some before it disappears."

"Are you sure?" I asked, offering Marvin the bowl one last time before I walked away.

He smiled. "I'm sure. Thank you."

I smiled at him as I turned and started walking toward the ring.

Daniel already had his gloves and head protection off, and he was making his way to the corner of the ring. I had glanced around the gym enough by now to realize that the girlfriend was nowhere in plain sight. I was unreasonably happy about this.

I carried the bowls of fruit, looking at Daniel but trying not to stare. He still didn't have on a shirt. I tried not to notice how perfect he was, but it was impossible. He might as well have been etched out of marble.

Billy was first in line at the corner, and he climbed through the ropes and hopped down to meet me. "Thank you," he said, reaching out to take one of the bowls out of my hand.

"You're welcome," I said.

I had come to stand beside my sister at the side of the ring. Billy leaned to the side to kiss Tess after he took the fruit from me. "Thank you," he said to her.

She was responding to him as I stepped back. I got out of the way so that Daniel could climb out of the ring. He came down the steps. I zigged when I should have zagged, and instead of stepping around me like he should have, Daniel collided with me.

"Whoa," I said, trying to get out of his way.

"I'm sorry, I'm sorry, my shirt's right over here." Daniel took the final step and lunged toward a nearby chair, the one with his shirt hanging over the back. It was a white t-shirt and I watched as he lifted it over his head, and stretched into it. He was damp with sweat and he had to bend and flex to get it on.

I wanted to blatantly stare, I really did, but I only let myself take glances. He was ridiculously gorgeous. I felt like some sort of joke was being played on me. I took a deep breath, staring into the bowl of fruit as he finished putting on his shirt.

"Sorry about that," he said, stepping toward me.

I reached out, offering him the bowl and thinking that it was no problem at all.

"Is that for me?" he asked.

"Yeah."

"Thank you," he said.

I smiled and nodded. I found it difficult to meet his eyes, but I did it. I glanced at him. His cheeks were ruddy and his hair was damp with sweat. His t-shirt was thin and it hugged his trim but substantial form. He looked like a super hero.

And then I had to go and look into his hazel green eyes, making my heart ache.

"Do you want to sit down for a minute?" he asked. He gestured to a bench that lined a nearby wall. It was basically just a long, painted plank of wood that was resting on top of a couple of pipes and bolted to the floor. But it was sturdy, and it was close enough to the wall that you could lean back.

We walked over to the bench, which was five or six steps away. Billy and Tess were closer to the ring, and a few people walked over to them to get a glimpse of the baby as they ate their fruit. I sat on the bench, looking at Tess and Billy instead of Daniel, who had come to sit beside me.

He set the bowl between us and he began working on removing his boxing gear. He had taken his gloves off in the ring, but his hands were still wrapped with fabric. Daniel began unwrapping. I wasn't looking at him, but I could see him doing it in my periphery.

"You must be finished training," I observed.

"I am. I'm *so* finished. Billy killed me just now."

"You held up," Billy said, hearing Daniel from several feet away. "You surprised me." Billy was talking around a mouth full of fruit, and he continued chewing as he glanced at us from over his shoulder.

Daniel gave Billy a thankful nod. "He's being kind," Daniel said. "I thought I was in shape. I am in shape. I'm just in a different kind of shape than Billy. Cardio is one thing, but it takes a certain kind of energy to hit something and to be hit. It's crazy. There's just nothing that will gas you out like boxing will."

Daniel used his toothpick and ate one, two, three bites of fruit in quick succession, popping them into his mouth and then chewing. Again, I was watching it all in my periphery.

"How long have you been up here?" I asked.

"Just a couple of hours," Daniel said. "Billy called me this morning and told me I should come by."

I glanced at him, nodding. I wanted to say something to respond about boxing, but all that came out of my mouth was, "Are you alone at the gym?"

He grinned. "Well, I'm with you now."

CHAPTER 7

I glanced at Daniel. He and I were sitting on a bench on the far side of the boxing ring at Marvin's gym. People were standing close by. We were not alone, yet no one was paying attention to us. I asked him if he was alone, and he answered me by saying he was with me since we were currently sitting on a bench together.

I made eye contact with him. As badly as I wanted to know where she was, I didn't want to press the subject of his missing girlfriend, so I dropped it.

"Did you do any boxing in the Army?"

"Do you mean in combat?" he asked.

I made a face as I thought about that. "No, I think I was imagining it happening like a brawl situation. You know, in movies, you always see military guys in bars, getting rowdy and getting in fights."

Daniel leaned back and laughed a little, eating more fruit. "A brawl?"

I shrugged. "I don't know. I thought a lot about what you might have done over there. I made up all sorts of stuff in my mind."

"I can't say that I was a part of a barroom brawl," he said shaking his head a little. "I messed around, fighting with my friends and stuff, but never any serious fistfights. And definitely no full rounds of sparring like Billy and I did just now. That was hard. We have a few bags on the base, but there's nothing like this gym or these guys."

"I came up here and did a few classes with Marvin when I was living in Galveston," I said.

"Did you?" Daniel pulled back to stare at me curiously, and I glanced his way, meeting his eyes.

I smiled and nodded. "I didn't hit anyone or get hit. I just punched those pads while Dizzy held them for me."

Daniel ate another bite of fruit, smiling at me.

How was it that I now loved the way he chewed?

"Did you like it?" he asked.

"Yes. Like what?"

"Boxing," he said.

"Oh, yeah. I did, actually. I probably would have stuck with it, you know, for exercise, if I didn't… move back home."

"Do you miss it?" he asked. "Galveston?"

"Yes," I replied without looking at him. "Very much. Especially now that little Tara's born. I wish I was close enough to see her more. This is only the third time I've seen her since she was born."

"That's still pretty good," he said. "At least you don't live in Georgia."

All sorts of thoughts got stuck in my head like a traffic jam as a result of his statement. One of them was that I wouldn't mind living in Georgia if it was with him. But I didn't let that come out of my mouth, thank goodness.

"Yeah," I said, nodding. "But even still, at least you're closer than Saigon."

"Yep," he agreed. "I'm a lot closer now."

We sat there for a minute in companionable silence while Daniel finished his fruit. It didn't take long for the other fighters to do the same. The whole big bowl that took us a half-hour to cut and fill was devoured in a matter of seconds.

It went back to business as usual in the gym. Marvin and two other guys got into the ring and started going over combinations and drills. Billy and Tess continued talking with people. They took Tara and headed toward the front of the gym.

"I expected to see you in your Army uniform," was the next thing I said to Daniel.

Daniel let out a chuckle. "You thought I'd be boxing in my fatigues?"

"No, not today. I'm talking about Thanksgiving. When you came into the house. I, I, I didn't know you were coming, but once I did find out, I instantly pictured you coming in wearing a green outfit—all decked-out."

"Wow, with the helmet and everything?"

"Yeah, boots too," I said. I smiled. "I guess I just thought you wore that every day now—like you're just an Army guy from now on."

Daniel let out a little laugh, leaning against the wall and sprawling his legs out comfortably in front of him. "Nope. I wear some of that stuff to work, but mostly I'm just a t-shirt kind of guy."

"How's the weather at Fort Benning?"

"About the same as here. It's cooler right now, but the summer is hot."

"Is it near the coast?" I asked, even though I had already looked at a map.

"Four hours to the Florida gulf coast. I've only been there once, but it's really pretty. It's different than it is here. The water is really blue over there."

"It's because of the Mississippi," I said. "It empties into the gulf, and the current comes this way, so everything to the east of it is blue, and everything to the west of it is brown."

I made an arching motion in mid-air with my hand, representing the gulf flowing in one direction.

Daniel nodded, looking at me like he was impressed I knew such a thing.

"Galveston's even bluer than a lot of the beaches in Louisiana," I continued. "Because it's further from the mouth of the Mississippi, and by the time the current gets here, a lot of that brown from the river has already dissipated."

Daniel nodded and thought silently for a few seconds. "I knew all that," he said, finally.

I leaned to the side and pushed at him with my shoulder. "Why'd you let me say it to you?" I asked.

"Because it was cute. You changed into a teacher. I felt like I was in your classroom for a second."

I laughed. "If you were in my real classroom, I'd teach you how to tie your shoe and say your ABC's. I have one boy, Ricky, in my class this year who can say it backwards."

"The ABC's?" Daniel asked, sounding disbelieving.

I nodded. "Yeah. It's something he practiced to impress everyone. He says other stuff backwards, too."

I had told Daniel some about my job when we talked on the phone a few months ago, but Ricky wasn't in my class back then.

"I didn't know six-year-olds practiced stuff," Daniel said. "I feel like I might have been an underachiever back then. When I was six, I was trying to catch lizards and throw rocks at barges."

I laughed. "I think his dad is into it," I said. "He told me about the backwards thing the first time we met."

"Who, the dad?" he asked.

"Yeah."

"I'll have to remember that," Daniel said. "I'll have to teach my son some kind of cool trick before he goes to school so he can impress his teacher."

"Where's your girlfriend?" I asked.

The comment about Daniel with a son sent me over the edge, and the question just came out of my mouth before I could stop it.

"Kelly left to go back to Georgia yesterday."

"Why so soon?" I asked. My heart buzzed and I hoped against hope that he would say they had a big falling out and broke up.

"That was the plan all along," he said. "She just came for Thanksgiving. Her dad's a pilot, and he came to pick her up on Friday. It's a short trip in a plane."

"How long was she here?"

"We drove in Wednesday. She stayed two nights, but really just one full day."

"I'm surprised Ms. Nancy let her stay the night at your house."

"She didn't," Daniel said. "Kelly stayed at Aunt Alma's next door."

"Oh," I said. I nodded, feeling some relief. "When are you going back?"

"Tomorrow. I'll leave early because I have to be back for work Monday morning."

"Bye-bye to the beard," I said, glancing at him.

This caused him to rub his face, which was a heavenly sight. I could not look away. I just stared, taking in his face and wondering how he had managed to become the most handsome man in the whole world. I ached to get back to those moments when he wanted me. It was a physical feeling of desperate yearning, and I was barely able to suppress it, barely able to refrain from leaning into Daniel, forcing him to catch me, hold me in his arms.

"It's not much of a beard, anyway," he said. "I've only been growing it a week or so."

"Well, I like it," I said. "But I bet I would like it both ways."

"Thank you," he replied.

I sighed and turned a little, propping my knee on the wooden bench. "Can you tell me one thing?"

"What do you mean?" he asked.

"Can you please share one thing with me about the war? I feel like you had to go through hard things, and I wasn't there for you."

Daniel hesitated as he thought for a moment. "There's a song," he said. "It's an American song, a pop hit that everybody likes. They were playing it all the time on American radio. It was coming over the loudspeakers when we made it back to the base. I was injured and had seen too much battle that day, people dying, and people in a lot of pain—most of them, I couldn't help. Some of them I could, but most of them I couldn't. It was by far the hardest day of my life. But anyway, this song was playing at just the wrong time in my delirious state, and it stuck in my head like a rusty nail. Now I can't hear it at all. I can't even listen to it for a few seconds. If it comes on the radio, I have to leave the room. If somebody even starts humming it, I feel sick to my stomach and start sweating. It makes me physically ill."

"What song is it?" I asked.

He shook his head with a little humorless smile. "I don't even want to say the name."

"Okay," I said, nodding. I sat quietly, not knowing quite what to say. I wanted to reach out and touch him, comfort him, care for him. I wanted to start a petition to have that song, whatever it was, stripped from the radio and banned for eternity.

"When are you heading back?" he asked.

"I don't know exactly. I have to work Monday morning, but I was thinking about staying here tomorrow and going to church with Tess and Billy. I haven't been in a while."

"To church at all, or are you talking about the one in Galveston?"

"The one in Galveston," I said. "If I miss more than two weeks back home, my mom hosts a prayer meeting for me."

Daniel laughed.

"Do you go?" I asked.

"Yeah," he said. "My mom stays on me about it, too. That was one of the first things she did when I told her I was going to stay in Georgia. She looked up churches and sent me a list."

"Did you stay there because of your girlfriend?" I asked.

"No," he said. "I was already planning on staying before we met."

It was the oddest thing. I hated talking about her, but at the same time, I wanted to continue to do it.

"Does she go to church?" I asked.

"Yes."

"What does she do?" I asked.

"For a job?" he asked.

I nodded.

"She grew up taking dance—tap and ballet and all that. She teaches a couple of classes at a dancing school."

I glanced at Daniel and found that he was looking at the boxing ring, absentmindedly watching the guys work as we talked.

"Does she live right there in Fort Benning?" I asked.

"Yeah, but it's big. It's like its own town."

"How does she get to live there if she's not in the military?"

"Her dad," Daniel said. "He's one of the main guys over there."

Of course he was. He was probably the head of the whole US Army. He was probably the President of the United States. He probably flew the presidential plane over here to pick up his daughter.

"I don't know if that's a good thing or a bad thing," I said.

"What do you mean?"

"Having your girlfriend's dad be your boss. On one hand, he could help you out, and on the other hand, you're kind of stuck."

"I'm not stuck in anything," he said. "I'm my own man."

I glanced at him. "She's pretty good, anyway. It's probably not such a bad thing to be stuck with her."

"Nobody's stuck," he said.

"I'm just saying… she's nice. She's obviously pretty. She got along with everybody at Thanksgiving. She seems good for you." I was trying to be nice. I was trying to be logical and not let my feelings factor into it.

"Do you think she's good for me?" he asked.

I glanced at him when he said it. We had both been looking at the action in the ring, but I shifted to stare at him, taking in the shapes of his profile.

"Don't you?" I said. "You must think so if you're bringing her to family dinners and stuff—holidays and everything." I tried to speak in a calm, measured tone, but I was nervous and I was almost certain it came across in my voice.

"I guess you're right," he said, resolutely. He looked my way. Our eyes met. "She's a good person," he said, holding the stare.

"Yeah. She's good for you."

"Yeah."

More staring.

"But if you ever figure out that she's not… that you're not… if you're ever not dating her anymore, I'm sure there's tons of girls who would really love..." I was so comically nervous about saying these things that I was relatively sure my last sentence didn't make much sense at all. I just sort of lost my breath and cut it off.

"Tons of girls who would love what?" he asked, smiling a little.

"Who, you know, would want to… marry you."

"Marry me?" he said with his eyebrows raised.

"Yeah."

"Not just date me, or go to Thanksgiving dinner with me?"

"I mean, that too, but marry you, too. Not that she's a bad choice, but you could obviously have any woman you would ever want."

Daniel stared at me. My heart pounded like it might jump out of my chest. I could actually feel the veins in my neck pumping blood as he regarded me. I tried to peel my eyes off of him, but I couldn't. I just stared back, shaking, feeling like a ticking time bomb.

"Nobody said I was marrying her," Daniel said with an easy sort of confidence that made me want to lean into him—collapse into his arms. I wholeheartedly wished it was okay for me to do that.

CHAPTER 8

Daniel

A month later
Almost Christmas (December 23rd)
Galveston Island, TX

By the time he made quick stops to gas up, eat, and use the restroom, it took Daniel fourteen hours to drive from Fort Benning to Galveston. He had left early that morning, and it was 7pm on a Saturday night when he made it to the island. It was a misty, balmy winter evening. The sun had set over an hour before, and Daniel drove off of the ferry into the foggy night air. He had grown up on this island, and the winter mist felt like home.

His parents were expecting him, but he drove down Bank Street before going to their house. There were some people in Carson's diner on the corner, but the rest of the block was quiet. Most of the businesses, including the hardware store and Marvin's gym, were closed for the evening.

Daniel kept going down Bank Street until he reached Billy's house on the corner of Bank and 17th. He wasn't sure why he stopped there, but he did. He noticed that their lights were on, and he went with his instinct and parked and walked up to their door.

Billy answered the door not long after Daniel knocked. He looked surprised, but he instantly reached out and took Daniel into his arms. "What are you doing in Galveston, my brother?"

"I came for Christmas," Daniel said.

"I thought you were staying in Georgia."

"I thought I was, too. I was supposed to work, but a couple of others ended up staying, so I got to leave."

Billy had invited Daniel inside as they were talking.

"It smells good in here," Daniel said.

"We just ate, and I've been baking a few things to take to Louisiana tomorrow. I made some cornbread, for the dressing. Then cookies, and now a cake."

"You're baking?" Daniel asked.

"Yeah, Tess made dinner, but she's already in there, painting. She's got the baby in there with her. I'm on baking duty for the rest of the evening."

"I didn't know you baked," Daniel said.

"I do. I cook a lot, actually. We trade off. I might even do more than half now that Tara's been born."

Daniel followed Billy to the kitchen as they talked.

"Are you hungry? We just put up the leftovers from dinner if you want some. It was really good. Tess made it."

"What is it?" Daniel asked.

"Chicken and rice," Billy said. "There's some green beans, too. Sit down and eat. I just put everything into the icebox right before you knocked. It's still warm."

"I need to call my mom if I'm going to sit and eat," Daniel said. "I told her I'd be here around dinner time. She'll be worrying about me."

"Are you just pulling into town?" Billy asked, looking at Daniel with newfound curiosity.

"Yeah. And I'm starving. I could probably eat what you give me and another meal at my mom's."

"Good. We have plenty. Sit down and eat." Billy gestured to the stool, and Daniel nodded.

"I will if you don't mind."

"I want you to. The girls are upstairs, and I was just sitting in here, waiting to take the cake out of the oven. How long do you get to stay? Through Christmas?"

"Yeah. Christmas is on a Monday, and I'll leave Tuesday morning."

"Short trip," Billy said.

"Yep."

"But, at least you get to come home."

"I know."

Billy skillfully scooped some of the rice mixture and green beans onto the plate and put a fork on the side before he slid it toward Daniel. "Do you want me to warm it up? I just put it in there, so think it's still pretty warm."

"No, thank you," Daniel said, staring at it. "It's fine like this. It looks delicious. I'm going to call home really quick before I eat."

There was a telephone right there in the kitchen. Daniel placed the call and had a short conversation with his dad where he explained that he'd be home in an hour or so.

"Where's your lady friend?" Billy asked when Daniel got off the phone.

"We broke up right after Thanksgiving."

"I know. You didn't tell me. I've talked to you two or three times since then, and you didn't mention it."

"How'd you know, then?"

"Your sister told me," Billy said.

"Laney? What's Laney doing talking about my personal life? That's not the kind of stuff I share. It was Kelly's idea to come here for Thanksgiving, or you guys might not have even known we were dating. The only reason I told them we broke up is because Mom asked me what she could get Kelly for Christmas."

"Why don't you talk to them about it?" Billy asked.

Daniel shrugged and took a bite of food. "I don't know. Like I said, I had just started seeing her, and we weren't even that serious. I wasn't ready to introduce her to family."

"Laney didn't seem too happy about the breakup."

"Yeah, she liked Kelly," Daniel said, after he chewed another bite. "She called me, begging me to ask Kelly to take me back. She wanted to help me make a plan. I think she just wanted to travel in Kelly's dad's plane."

"I'm sure she did," Billy said. "Was it *his* plane, or does he just pilot it?"

"No, it's his. They're loaded. They have old money. His ancestors own a lot of land near Atlanta. They're descendants of Henry Ford or something. He's just in the military because he loves it."

"Wow," Billy said. "Now *I* kind of want to take a trip in Kelly's dad's plane."

Daniel laughed at that as he continued to chew. "This is really good," he said. "Thank you."

"You're welcome. So, what are you doing for Christmas? Are you just staying here with your parents?"

"Yeah, like I said, it was kind of last minute that I got to come home. What are you and Tess doing?"

"We leave tomorrow morning to go to her parents'. We'll spend the night there and wake up Christmas Day to open presents with them. I'm sure we'll come home later that afternoon—just make it a quick trip. I know I'm coming home, Tess might stay and get a ride back after a day or two. I have to get back into the gym with that match coming up next month."

"Oh, okay, but y'all won't be here on Christmas Day?" Daniel asked.

"Yeah, no. We'll be in Louisiana. Her parents and Abigail are there, and they've got grandparents and cousins that'll come over tomorrow night for Christmas Eve dinner. That's what all this is for," Billy said, gesturing to the baking that was taking place.

Daniel's mind didn't go to baking. His thoughts came to a screeching halt once Billy said her name. Abigail. His Abby. He loved the sound of her name, and hearing it brought to his mind all sorts of memories of her. He had known her for over four years, and there had never been a moment, during all that time, that he wasn't madly in love with her.

The first and second times he ever saw her was through a window, and that seemed to be a metaphor for their relationship. He could interact with her and see all of her true colors, but there was some invisible force between them, some boundary that had been put there by her and not him.

It wasn't there when he saw her at Thanksgiving, and that was the very thing that resulted in him breaking up with Kelly. He didn't know if the boundary would be back between them the next time he saw Abby. He didn't know if they could ever be together because of that. But seeing her at Thanksgiving and experiencing the feelings she gave him made him know that he had to break up with Kelly. It just wasn't fair to Kelly that he was capable of loving another woman so much. He had to work through his unresolved feelings for Abby before he could be with anyone else.

He didn't call Abby right away after he broke up with Kelly. He needed time to think about everything and establish his feelings and boundaries. He was busy at the base, anyway, and Christmas had come quickly.

He had hoped to try to accidentally run into Abby while he was in Galveston. He thought she might go there now that Tess had the baby. But it didn't seem like things were going to work out that way.

"I was hoping to run into Abby," he said to Billy. It was the main thing on his mind, so he wasn't surprised that it came out.

Billy looked at him. "What do you mean run into her? Are you trying to see her for Christmas? You could just come over there with us." Billy shrugged. "I'm sure you don't feel like making another trip after you just got here, but you're welcome to go with us in the morning."

"Oh, no, thanks. Thanks anyway. I wasn't trying to force anything. I was kind of hoping, you know, if it happens, it happens."

"No, I don't know," Billy said, staring blankly at Daniel. "It seems like if you wanted to talk to Abigail, you should just pick up the phone and call her. Or come with us. She'd love to see you. If that's what you're worried about, there's no need. She would really love to see you, I can promise you that."

"What makes you say that?"

"My wife," Billy said. "Tess talks to her all the time. She's doing something with letters to soldiers."

"Who?"

"Abby."

"What about letters?"

"Something about getting her students to write letters and do art projects to mail to soldiers overseas." Billy shrugged. "You can't tell me that's not about you."

"I didn't know anything about it," Daniel said.

"Well, I guess not if you never see her or talk to her." Billy was being casual but direct. "As far as any of us knew, you were with someone else."

"Has she said anything about me?" Daniel asked.

"Tess would know more, but yeah, I do know she talks about you to her sister."

"What does she say?" Daniel asked, sitting up and getting to the edge of his chair.

"You'll have to ask Tess."

"Ask me what?" Tess said, coming into the room without either of them hearing her.

"About your sister," Billy said.

"What about her?" Tess asked, smiling as she crossed to Daniel. She gave him a hug. "I didn't know you were coming over," she said, unintentionally changing the subject as she came up to him.

"I didn't know either. It was a last-minute trip."

"He was asking about your sister," Billy said. "I was telling him that Abby would love to see him."

"Yeah, she would looove to see you," she said it in a slow, dramatic, dazed tone and Daniel tilted his head curiously at her. "She would love to see you," Tess repeated, being a little more serious. "She really would. She'd probably get in her car and head this way if she knew you were sitting here right now."

Daniel let out a little laugh. "If she did that, I would sit right here till she got here," he said, joking around, but feeling serious.

"Are you saying you want me to call her?"

Daniel's chest tightened at the thought.

"Where's Tara?" Billy asked.

"I just fed her. She's laying in her crib for a minute while I came to get some water. Would you like some water?" she continued, looking at Daniel. "I see you got a bite of rice."

"It was tasty, Tess, thank you," Daniel said distractedly.

"You're welcome. I'll make you some water." Tess was already in the process of making her own water, so it was nothing to add another glass. "I was being serious about my sister, though," she added. "Billy told me he thought you might have broken up with that girl from Georgia."

"I did," Daniel said.

"Well, I didn't want to interfere, especially since Billy hadn't heard it from you, so I didn't mention it to my sister. I knew you would call her if you wanted to. But, yeah, if she knew you were… unattached, she'd probably be pretty happy about that. I think it's fair to say she'd be happy."

It was a fairly vague statement, but Daniel felt a wave of pleasure and hope as a result of it. He was happy, and at the same time, he was scared of going through all the trouble of driving to Louisiana if he wasn't a hundred percent sure about where Abby stood.

"I don't know," he said. "As much as I'd like to pick up and go over there with you guys, I'd basically be doing a one-eighty on my mom about this whole trip. I was sort of just hoping to run into Abby while I was here, that way I could try to gauge where she stood."

"I'll tell you right now where she stands," Tess said.

"Where?" Daniel asked.

"Wherever you're standing," she said.

She was being totally serious.

"Nu-uh," Daniel said, grinning a little and shaking his head at her.

"Yes-huh," Tess said. "She does this whole thing with her class writing letters to soldiers, and I know it's because of you. They wrote an article about it in the Lake Charles American Press. She's got other teachers doing it." Tess set her glass down and lifted her hands in a sincere gesture of surrender. "Look, I totally understand about not having time to go to Louisiana on this trip, and ultimately it's up to you whether you want to try to talk to Abigail or not, but I do know she'd be really excited to hear from you, Daniel. There's just no question about that."

Daniel nudged his chin toward the telephone that was mounted on the wall nearby. "Call her and see what she says about me," he said.

Tess smiled. "What are we in seventh grade?"

"Just do it," Billy said.

He was whipping his hand around excitedly. He was so wound up and intense about it that Tess laughed. "What do you want me to do? Ask if she'll come here right now? Because I bet she would."

"No, don't do that. I don't want her to miss Christmas with your family. Maybe it's too rushed this time. Maybe I'll be able to come for longer in the summer. I might even be moving back."

"So, do you want me to call her, or just wait?" she asked.

Daniel shrugged. "I don't know. I'm not sure since she wasn't planning on coming here. Let me think about it."

CHAPTER 9

Abigail

The following day
Christmas Eve

There would be around twenty family members coming to my parents' house for dinner on Christmas Eve. Mom and I had been cooking and baking for two days in preparation for it. It was after 5pm and getting close to time for it to happen.

Every heating appliance in the house was in full use as we tried to get everything warm for dinner at 6pm when everyone arrived.

Billy and my grandma were watching Tara in the living room while Tess, Mom, and I finished the food preparation in the kitchen. The phone rang, and my mom was closest to it, so she reached out and answered it.

"Hello, Merry Christmas, Cohen residence. (She paused.) Oh, why, thank you. Yes, yes, I do. (Pause.) I will. You too. She's right here. Okay. You too. Hang on." My mother smiled as she held the phone out to me.

"Who is it?" I said the words so quietly that I might as well have been mouthing them.

My mom shook the phone, urging me to take it from her.

"Who is it?" I asked again as I reached for the receiver.

"Long distance," she whispered with wide eyes, telling me to hurry up and talk.

"Hello?" I said, having no idea who would be on the other end.

"Hey, Abby."

He said only two words, but I instantly knew who he was. Daniel.

I tried not to react outwardly. I stared blankly at the countertop, zoning out and not caring at all what my mom and sister were doing.

"Hey," I said. "Daniel?"

"Yeah."

"What are you doing?" I asked.

My heart pounded, and every second that he paused before he replied seemed like an eternity.

"I'm at my parents' house in Galveston. I'm up at the hardware store, actually."

"It's not open, is it?"

"No, I'm just up here by myself. I came by so I could give you a call. I was talking to Tess and Billy yesterday about your plans. They said you were eating Christmas Eve dinner with your family. I was hoping to catch you before you all sat down for dinner."

"Yeah, yeah, you did. Nobody is eating yet. We're still waiting on a few to get here," I said. "Are you staying in Galveston through Christmas? They didn't even tell me you were home."

"Yeah, I'm here, but I have to get back to Fort Benning right after Christmas. It'll be a quick trip. I thought I might run into you in Texas, but Tess said you were staying at your mom's this year."

"Yeah, we usually do Christmas here," I said, widening my eyes at Tess for not telling me she and Daniel had a conversation about me. She was looking at me, and she shrugged innocently because she had no idea what Daniel was saying on the phone.

"I know you're about to have people over and everything. I won't keep you. I just wanted to—"

"No, no, it's fine," I said, desperately not wanting him to hang up. "Tess didn't tell me you came home. I'm so happy you did, and that you called. Both. My family's all over the place, but we have another phone... in the den... if you... wanted to talk for a little while. Or not. I didn't know why you were calling. Did you say that already?"

I was nervous and rambling, and my mom and sister were standing in earshot. But I didn't care. I just wanted to say the right things to Daniel.

"Tell Daniel we have plenty of food if he wants to come over here," Mom said from the other side of the sink.

"Thanks," I said. "He knows. My mom said you're welcome over here, but you already know that. I hope you do."

"Would it be possible for us to talk a little later?" Daniel asked. "Maybe after your dinner? Are you spending the night at your mom's?"

"Yes. Of course. Yes, I am staying here, and please. I'd love to talk. What time?"

"Would nine or so give you time to finish up with your family?"

"Yes. Of course."

"Okay, I'll call from the hardware store. I have to come back up here after dinner to help Randall build a couple of toys for his kids—a dollhouse and a rocking horse."

"You're building those things tonight?" I asked, smiling.

"Yes, with Randall."

"Who are you, Santa Claus?"

Daniel laughed. "Randall ordered them through Dad's wholesale catalogue, and he just figured out there was assembly required. I'll tell him we need to be done by nine so I can call you."

"Actually, if it—never mind."

"What?"

"I was just going to say we could do ten," I said. "It might be quieter here and that would give you more time, but it doesn't matter. That might be kind of late."

"No, we can do ten," he said. "That way I don't have to rush with those toys. I don't really know what I'm in for."

"Okay, that sounds incredible," I said.

"Yeah it does. I'll call you at ten o'clock tonight."

"Great," I said.

"Great. At this number?"

"Yes."

"Okay. Bye."

"Bye."

I smiled when I hung up the phone.

"Is he coming over?" Mom asked.

"No ma'am."

"It sounded like that was what you were saying."

"No. He was talking about calling me. He's planning on calling back later tonight."

"What'd he say?" Tess asked.

"Pretty much just that. He said he knew I was busy but that he wanted to call back… and he talked about helping Randall put together toys, but that really only had to do with calling later…"

I trailed off when I heard noise at the front door. Someone had come in. I could hear commotion and people exclaiming. I knew it was my aunt and her family.

"Did he tell you he broke up with that girl in Georgia?" Tess asked.

"I wish," I said, letting out a humorless laugh.

"No, he did. I was just asking if he told you about it."

"What?" I said, staring at Tess like I couldn't understand what she was saying. Because I couldn't.

"Daniel broke up with that girl. He told us."

"Why didn't you tell me?" I asked, feeling stunned. "Did he really?"

Tess nodded.

"They're all-the-way broke up?"

Tess nodded again.

"Why wasn't that the first thing you told me?" I asked.

"Because I knew you wouldn't get to see him on this trip, anyway."

"I have to go," I said instantly. "I have to go over there."

"Go where?" Mom asked in a motherly tone.

"To Galveston." I looked at my sister. "Tonight."

"What?" she asked, staring at me.

I nodded. "I want to be there by ten, so that means I can still stay here and eat dinner and everything. I can leave as late as seven and still make it."

"What would you do at ten o'clock at night?" Mom asked.

"Surprise Daniel," Tess answered.

"Are you going to try to drive there and back in one night?" Mom asked.

"I'll just spend the night at Tess and Billy's if they don't mind."

"We don't mind at all, but that's a big house for you to be in by yourself. I usually have Mom come stay the night with me if Billy's got to be out of town."

"It's fine," I said. "It's safe. I'll sleep upstairs."

This was a true testament to how badly I wanted to go. Under normal circumstances, I would've been scared out of my wits to stay by myself at Tess and Billy's house. I had always lived with my parents or had a roommate.

"I'm fine with it," Tess said. "Just be careful driving in the dark."

"I will. I'll be fine."

"I'm not fine with it," Mom said. "What about Christmas?"

"I'll see," I said. "I might drive back tomorrow. I'll have to see what Daniel is… I'll call you and let you know."

"Oh my goodness, are you really driving over there tonight?" Tess asked.

"Yes," I said, nodding. "Absolutely." I tilted my head at Tess. "If you're sure he's not with that girl anymore."

"He's not. I just talked to him yesterday."

I leaned over and took my sister by the face, holding her cheeks. I scrunched up my face and kissed her on the forehead. "I love you," I said, bursting with excitement. "I don't know why that news about Daniel wasn't the first thing out of your mouth when you saw me, but I still love you for telling me now." I reached up and gently slapped her cheeks after I did all that, a few tiny, little patting slaps. She laughed at my excitement.

"Who's cooking? It smells good in here!"

My aunt came around the corner, and after that, everything got loud and busy in the kitchen. Before I knew it, we had eaten and were talking about doing our annual gift exchange. I tried not to be obvious about it, but I was in a hurry. It felt rushed for me to leave the party at seven, but I knew I had to in order to make it to the hardware store in time.

I told my family that I loved them but I had to be going. I hugged several of them on my way out, not offering any information about where I was headed. I figured Mom and Tess could run interference for me once I left. I stopped at my apartment to throw some clothes in a bag and pick up a present I wanted to give to Daniel.

I stopped again in Beaumont to fill up my tank with gas. I drove a little MG Midget, and I had made the trip to Galveston several times in it. I knew where all the gas stations were, and I knew I could make it a long way without having to stop again.

I had left my house in such an excited haze that it took me all the way to that gas station in Beaumont to figure out that this was an extremely crazy stunt for me to pull.

First of all, I had to hope and pray that Daniel would be happy to see me.

The whole thing about him not having a girlfriend could be hearsay. My unannounced arrival could turn out to be an unwanted or awkward encounter. I figured if that happened, I could always lie and say I was in Galveston for a different reason—like picking up a Christmas present that Tess and Billy accidentally left behind.

Was I really making up backup lies? I told myself it wouldn't come to that. But it didn't stop me from playing out all sorts of scenarios as I drove.

Secondly, and perhaps the craziest part of it all was that if things worked out with Daniel, which I obviously hoped they would, then I would be sleeping at Tess's house in Galveston. I would be spending the whole night alone, and waking up, also alone, in a huge, empty house on Christmas morning.

Several times, I thought of turning back. Daniel had no idea I was coming. It would be more than reasonable for me to turn around. My family would love that, actually, since I would make it back for Christmas. I came up with all kinds of reasons why going to Galveston was a bad idea.

But the second I would start to doubt myself, I would think of Daniel and how he was right there, just a couple of hours from me.

I was pulled to him.

There was just no question that I was going.

CHAPTER 10

It was twenty-till-ten when I finally pulled into my parking spot on Bank Street in front of the hardware store. Randall's truck was parked next to Daniel's, and I saw, after I parked, that Randall was sitting in it. He waited for me to get out of my car and approach the store, and he rolled down his window to yell at me.

"I was wondering who that was in an MG!" he said. "What are you doing here? You lost or something?"

"No, I was coming to pick up some nails."

"Oh, well, they don't have the... it's just Daniel in there, and he doesn't even have the register open..." Randall stopped talking once he saw me smiling and he realized I had been joking about the nails.

"I just came to say 'hi' to Daniel. I saw his truck."

"Oh, yeah, well, he's in there. He was back in the office when I left."

I nodded and waved at him as I walked toward the door. "Merry Christmas," I said from over my shoulder.

"Merry Christmas," he yelled.

The front of the hardware store was lined with windows, so I could easily see inside as I went through the door. The bell dinged when I opened the door, and I looked across the store, peering toward the office.

"Did you forget something?" I heard Daniel's voice yelling from the office, and I hunched over, ducking and curling my shoulders as if that would hide me from anything. I didn't want to answer him, so I just jogged toward his voice. I padded silently on my toes, taking long, leaping, quiet strides across the hardware store toward the office.

The lights were low. It wasn't dark in there, but it certainly wasn't as well-lit as it was while the store was open. The office light was on, though, and I headed that way.

"Randall?" I heard Daniel's voice from way closer than I thought it would be. He must have been right at the door of the office, because as I approached, I heard his voice like it was only a few feet away.

I came to a screeching halt, stopping outside the door so that I wouldn't run right into him. I was out of breath from adrenaline and from running, and I smiled at myself as I tried to take silent, gasping breaths to get my breathing under control.

"Hello?"

Daniel's deep voice was emotionless and it projected into the store. He didn't hear me. He stepped out of the office like he was planning on going to the door to see who had come in. I was standing to his left as he walked out, and his focus shifted toward me. His eyes landed on mine in what seemed like an instant. I saw as he recognized me and then his face shifted to one of happy surprise.

"Abby?"

I let out a breathless laugh at the way he said my name and the fact that I was still holding my breath from jogging.

I waved. "Hi."

Daniel glanced around briefly before meeting my eyes again. He had on dark jeans and a grey t-shirt that had an Army logo on it. It fit him tightly, hugging his chest, and the sight of him standing so close with that big, broad chest was too much to take in. I glanced away.

"Hi," he said as soon as I looked away. "I was just about to call you."

My eyes met his again, and I smiled. "I'm not there," I said.

"I see that," he said, seriously. "You're here."

"Yeah. I was just passing by, and I saw your truck out front. Randall said you were in the office, so I thought I'd come in."

"You were passing by?" he asked.

I nodded, staring up at him, flirting with him.

"What are you doing in my hardware store and not in Louisiana?"

I shrugged, staring into his multi-colored eyes. "I just thought maybe we could… talk in person instead of… on the telephone. You know, so no one has to pay for long distance."

"Oh, so you were just trying to save money?"

"Yeah," I said, nodding.

"Come here," he said, smiling. Daniel reached out and took me into his arms, hugging me. It was a confident embrace like a friend or family member would give you. I didn't care. I would take what I could get.

I held him back, molding my body to him, holding on for dear life. I hugged him for several long seconds before we broke the contact and stepped back. I hadn't remembered to breathe while we were hugging, and I took a deep breath before I spoke.

"I, I just was thinking after you called. I decided I'd come stay the night at Tess and Billy's since I knew you'd be at the store with Randall. I thought maybe I could run into you. I was trying to find you so we could… talk for a minute in person." I took another deep, unsteady breath, stretching my arms since I didn't know what to do with my hands. "Also, Tess mentioned that you weren't dating that other person anymore, so I thought, I don't know, that you wouldn't get in trouble for talking to me." I paused before adding, "Are you, though?"

"Am I what?" he asked.

"Still dating. Or broken up."

"I'm only one of those."

"Broken up?" I asked hopefully.

"Yes."

"For how long have you been?"

"Since Thanksgiving."

I had to fight a huge grin that threatened to cover my face. I bit the inside of my lip.

"Can we go somewhere?" I said to distract him from my joy over his breakup. "Or we could sit in there for a while." I gestured to the office. "Or we could go to Billy's." I shrugged. "We'd be comfortable at Tess and Billy's. And that way, when you have to leave, I won't have to go to the house by myself. I'll already be there."

"You are way too scared to sleep in that house by yourself," Daniel said, knowing my fear of the dark.

"I know," I said. "I kind of figured that out around Beaumont, but I just... kept driving."

"You would be up *all night* if you stayed at that house by yourself," Daniel said, smiling.

"Yeah," I answered, nodding dazedly.

"And that was your plan?" he asked, staring at me seriously.

"Yeah," I said, nodding again. "I still stand by it," I added, straightening my shoulders.

Daniel smiled at me. "What about Christmas?"

I shrugged. "I figured if you were busy, I'd just leave in the morning and go back home. It's not that far. Tess and Billy would still be there if I get an early start. Plus, most of the big stuff with my extended family and everything was done tonight."

"Did you miss it to come here?"

"I was there for most of it," I said. "Some of it. But all of that, Daniel, leaving there, coming here, sleeping scared… it's all no big deal at all. I wanted to do it, and I really feel like it's worth it if you'll just… talk to me… be willing to talk to me for a minute."

Daniel crossed his arms in front of his chest as he regarded me. His arms and chest were bulging, and at first, I thought he was showing off for me, but then I realized that was just how he looked—gorgeous in his resting position. He wasn't flexing or trying to show off, his arms were just glorious and distracting on their own.

"I think I would love to sit somewhere and talk to you, Abigail."

My eyes met his when he said my name—it was more that he said that version of my name. Daniel had been the first and main person to call me Abby. He was the one who started it. I was almost sure I had never heard him call me Abigail, now that I thought about it."

"You just called me Abigail," I said.

"I did," he said.

"What made you do that?"

"I don't know. I just wanted to."

"Are you mad at me?" I asked.

He smiled and reached out to hug me again. "Why would I be mad?" he asked giving me a reassuring squeeze.

I didn't say any more about it. I just enjoyed the hug.

We decided to leave right after that. We knew we would be more comfortable at Tess and Billy's house than at his dad's office, so we locked up and headed down Bank Street. He followed me in his truck, and we both parked in their driveway. I brought a painting with me, which I held, but I also had a bag, and Daniel carried it inside for me.

We turned on a few lights, and he set my bag down at the foot of the stairs. I was holding the framed painting, and instead of leaving it there with my other things, I carried it with me to the living room and carefully rested it in one of the chairs, facing out.

It was a beach scene that Tess had captured the very first day we moved to Galveston. It had a depiction of me sitting on a towel on the sand. Tess had painted me in several of her paintings over the years, and most of the time, I just looked like a female in the distance. Rarely could you tell who I was. The same was true with this painting. It was a female form with all the right shapes and shadows, but if you didn't know it was me, you would just think it's a painting of some girl on the beach.

It had always been my favorite painting. Her style had developed and changed over the years. Looking at her current work with this one side-by-side, you could see where she had improved. But it was a charming scene, and it definitely had sentimental value to me.

I brought it with me so I could give it to Daniel as a Christmas present. I didn't know what would come of this night, but I knew he would like it and appreciate it as a gift.

"Come sit," I said, gesturing to the couch after I situated the painting in a chair. "Can I get you something to drink or eat?"

"I'm fine," Daniel said. He just stood there looking at me for a few seconds before he went to the couch. "What's the painting about?" he asked.

"It's me," I said. "It's the first one Tess did when we moved here."

"I know what it is, I was just wondering why it was here."

He kicked off his shoes near the coffee table and then sat in the corner of the couch. He cocked his leg up beside him, looking like he wasn't in a hurry. The sight of his relaxed demeanor absolutely delighted me. I sat beside him.

"I just had it with me," I said, not being specific about the painting quite yet. "You're not dating anyone are you? I mean, I know you broke up with the girl from Georgia... but it hit me on the way over here that I should ask and make sure you weren't dating anyone. You know, anyone... else."

Daniel stared at me with an irresistible cautious smile. "Why do you want to talk about if I'm single or not?"

I was breathless and shaken, and I tried to calm my nerves and steady my voice as I spoke. I felt shy and vulnerable, humbled, like I wanted to just curl up at his feet and beg him to forgive me, to love me again.

Cautiously, I scooted slightly closer. "Because I'm trying to sit here and talk to you. I'm trying to sit kind of close to you and tell you things."

"What do you want to say?" Daniel asked. And as he asked the question, he reached out for me. It was the first time he had reached out for me in a way that felt tender, and I took full advantage of it. I went to him. I tucked my head onto his chest, curling up beside him and trying to get as close to him as possible while he was giving me an opening. He responded to me, shifting and moving in all the right ways to help me get closer and settle in next to him.

My body was alive with sensation. I so desperately wanted to be close to Daniel that the reality of it happening was electric. I was so filled with excitement and anticipation that I felt a slight pulsing, electrical feeling in my body as we touched. I tucked my head into his chest, curling up and holding onto him tightly.

"The painting's for you," I said, without looking at him. "I brought it with me to give you for Christmas. Sorry I didn't get to wrap it."

"You're giving me that?" he said.

"Yes."

"It's your favorite."

"You're my favorite," I said.

"What's changed with you, Abby?" he asked, still holding onto me.

I took a minute to think about my answer. "I don't know," I said, honestly. "I realized too late that you were wonderful, I think. If I could do it, I would go back to a long time ago and make myself feel then like I feel now. I don't know what I was thinking. I don't know how I didn't see it. I don't blame you at all if you can't forgive me or get close to me anymore. I would totally understand. I just want you to know I'm sorry and that I do think you're amazing. I do still want to be your friend, and of course, I wanted to give you the painting."

Daniel took a deep breath. My face was resting near his chest, and I felt it rise and fall. He reached up and rubbed his face. I wasn't looking at his face, but I could see him in my periphery and feel what he was doing.

"I heard you have your students writing letters," he said.

I pulled back just enough to stare up at him. My face was near his jaw.

"I do," I said. "We've written and sent over two hundred, and that's just at our school. Other schools are joining us now." I smiled. "We hear back from the soldiers. That's the best part. They thank the kids and even draw them pictures. Everybody's been so nice and thankful."

"How'd you know where to send them?"

"I called the operator and asked for the United States Army office. I had to leave messages and talk to three different people, but I have an address I send them to now, and they get them to soldiers."

"You could always write me one and send it to Georgia if you get bored."

"I've already done that. I just don't mail them."

"Already done what? Written me a letter?"

"A lot of them," I said. I shrugged and squirmed, feeling shy after I said that. "I just responded to you," I said. "I had most of your old letters, and I just, responded to them all. The way they should have been responded to in the first place. I wished I had treated them with care before." I shrugged again. "It's probably silly, but it made me feel better to go back and read them and do it differently this time."

"When do I get to read what you wrote?" he asked.

I let out a little laugh. "Never."

"Why not?"

"Because. Just no. I honestly didn't think I would ever even tell you I wrote them."

"Well, you did tell me, so now you have to let me read them."

I laughed silently, thinking of all the embarrassingly honest things I had written. "I actually have no idea why I told you that just now. I should've known you would want to read them, and there's just no way I can let you."

CHAPTER 11

"Why not?" Daniel asked, pulling back even more so that he could stare down at me.

I smiled. I had never felt so content as I did right then, sitting in his arms with him staring down at me.

"I can't let you," I said shaking my head. "Not yet, at least."

"What's that mean?"

"It means I was just far too… raw… and honest to let you… they were really… I don't know… sentimental."

I reached out and put my hand on his arm. "I don't know why I told you about those," I said. "They're embarrassing."

He shifted and put his hand on my head, holding me close. I leaned into him.

"Just tell me one thing," he said.

"What?" I asked.

"You pick," he said.

"Out of what?" I asked.

Daniel laughed at me for not getting what he was saying. "Your letters," he said. "Tell me one thing you said to me in them."

"Oh, just one thing?" I asked, contemplating. "Uh, you had told me about your friend from Tennessee, David, who has a pond with ducks, and when I wrote back, I told you about my grandma's brother who had a duck farm. We used to go over there for New Year's every year when I was little. I'd take some rubber boots with me, and I'd go in the duck yard, as we called it. I'd stay out there all morning, just me and the ducks. They lived in Kinder, which is only like an hour or two away, but it seemed like a whole vacation to go and see them every year."

"That's not personal or embarrassing at all," Daniel said, sounding disappointed.

I laughed at him.

"Really," he said. "You should just let me read them if they're for me, anyway."

"I'll think about it," I said. I sat up, adjusting and turning to look at him. "But just know that I did take the time to respond to each of your letters. Finally."

"You responded to me the first time," he said.

"I did, but I'd do it way differently if I could go back." I looked at him and smiled a little. "But all I can do is try my best from here."

I was gently wrapped in his arms, and I stayed there for the next hour. We talked about all sorts of things. I had my head on his chest, not even looking at him as we talked. I could hear his deep voice differently that way, and it was soothing to my ears.

Finally, we got off the couch, but it was only so that Daniel could call his mom and tell her he wasn't coming home. He would sleep downstairs on the couch, and I would stay upstairs in the spare bedroom. Daniel offered to stay the night so that I wouldn't be frightened, and I didn't hesitate to take him up on it. He was a grown man, so his parents didn't question him about it—he was just calling to let them know where he was so they wouldn't worry. I heard him tell his mom he'd be home sometime late morning, and my heart ached, assuming we'd be parting ways at that point.

We made a snack and some drinks while we were in the kitchen, but within minutes, we headed to the living room to settle onto the couch again.

I grabbed a heavy cotton blanket out of the closet on my way back over there, and I curled up in it, spreading it across Daniel's lap once I was sitting next to him. He was being a gentleman—giving me space, but I could tell that he wanted me close to him. He responded by pulling me in every time I got close.

Some of the time we sat next to each other, and other times, I adjusted, leaning on him where he held onto me. We never kissed. We hardly even looked at each other. We just talked and let our bodies rest next to each other.

It was a little difficult to stay neutral at times because I felt such an intense physical response to Daniel. I wanted to kiss him more than I had ever wanted to kiss any other man in the whole world.

I wanted to kiss Daniel King more than I wanted to kiss Jim Morrison. He had passed away recently, but even if I was looking straight at Jim Morrison in his prime, I would still choose Daniel.

I wanted to kiss Daniel King and no one else for the rest of my life. It was insane for someone like me to feel this way, but honestly, the thought of anyone but Daniel was revolting. I knew in my heart that I would never want anyone else. I knew I would treat him right and never hurt him again. It seemed like he was going to be willing to let me prove that to him.

We sat on the couch and talked for another long stretch of time. It was after one o'clock in the morning when I sat up and stretched.

"It's Christmas!" I said with quiet, sleepy excitement. "Merry Christmas!"

"So far it's my best Christmas ever," he said.

I smiled. "And you're just an hour into it."

He grinned back at me, reaching out to touch my leg. I had been sitting with him for hours, and I still felt an electrical sensation when he touched me.

"What are you doing tomorrow?" I asked, thinking he might be about to leave.

"Christmas with my family," he said. "My mom makes a big meal and we have everyone over for lunch—my grandparents and aunts and cousins. There's twenty or thirty people. You've been over before. You know how it is."

"Yeah."

"Why were you asking?" he asked.

"I was just kind of wondering what I was going to do. I didn't want to come by if... I didn't know if your family would... "

"My family knows you," he said.

"I know, but I've never..." I trailed off, letting out a sigh since I was too shy to finish that sentence.

Daniel reached up and smoothed a lock of hair near my face. He tucked it behind my ear, causing a warm rushing sensation to happen in my gut.

"You've never what? he asked.

I was too shaken up to do anything but tell the truth. "I've never encountered them when I... when I lo-o-ve their son." I said the word so slowly that it almost didn't even sound like the word anymore."

"Did you just say you love me, Abigail Cohen?"

I bit my lip and nodded shyly, looking away.

"You didn't say it to me. You just said it about me."

"What?"

He gave me a squeeze. "You said it about me and not to me."

My eyes met his, but then I stared at his mouth and chin, then my eyes roamed down to his neck and chest. I gently placed my hand on his chest.

"I'm too scared to say it to you."

"Why?"

"Because I don't know how you feel about me."

Daniel was quiet for long enough that I glanced at him. He had a grip on me, and he pulled me to him, leaning down, to the place where his mouth was only an inch or two from mine. I leaned toward him just far enough that our lips were almost touching. There was barely any space between us. I was sharing the same breath as Daniel King, and nothing in my whole life had ever brought me as much pleasure. In that moment, I could have just melted away into helpless bliss.

"It's always only been you, Abby," Daniel said, staring at me. "I don't know how you do it, but you are the only woman in this whole world who can make me want you like this. For me to say *I love you* would not be enough. I have never not loved you. You are the one my heart returns to, no matter what. I would drop anything at any time to be with you."

We were so close that he clearly saw my eyes fill with tears as he spoke.

I didn't care that I didn't deserve him.

"I love you," he added, plain as day and with no reservations. "There's no question about that."

I kissed him.

I was the one who made the move. I leaned in, letting my lips make glorious contact with his. They just barely touched. It was so delicate and gentle that I could feel Daniel take a slow, measured breath. His hands gripped me slightly, but he was being as gentle as he could. I could feel the tension he tried to hold back. His muscles were tense. I licked my lips and then leaned in and kissed him again. My lips slid against his, and his grip tightened as he pulled me closer.

Our kisses were gentle. Over and over again, he tested and probed, gentle but quick kisses, one after another. I thought Daniel would be inexperienced, but he kissed me with a sweet sort of confidence that surprised me and drove me wild with desire.

We kissed lightly like that for several minutes. I had wanted to connect with him so desperately and for so long, that I was urgent and hungry for this kiss to deepen.

I tried to hold back, but it was difficult. I opened my mouth, hoping he would respond, and he did. Daniel tilted his head the next thing I knew, I felt a glorious intrusion into my mouth. His tongue was warm and silky, and I moved and adjusted to let him in, taste more of him.

His kiss was patient, gentle, warm and soft, and yet deep, thrilling, and passionate. Our connection remained urgent and needy for a while before Daniel finally pulled back.

Both of us took a second to catch our breath we sat in silence, staring at each other from only inches apart. We stayed there for what must have been a full minute. I had no idea what he was thinking.

"I love you," was the first thing I said. I touched the side of his handsome perfect face. "I love you, Daniel."

He leaned back into the corner of the couch, glancing at the ceiling, stretching out, and smiling like he was living the good life. He made me repeat that two more times.

I had every intention of going upstairs to sleep, but we stayed up until 4am, and I fell asleep next to him on the couch. I woke up with my head on his lap. His legs were hanging off of the edge of the couch. I woke up lying on my side, positioned where I was staring at his knees. He still had on jeans.

I blinked a few times, taking in my surroundings and remembering where I was. My heart was content and peaceful waking up next to Daniel. I felt happy and whole.

There was enough light in the house that I knew it was morning. I blinked, focusing on Daniel's pants. I realized that he must have slept sitting up. I shifted to stare upward, turning my head gently so I wouldn't wake him up… but he was already awake, staring down at me.

"Good morning, sunshine."

"Good morning, my Daniel," I said sleepily.

I turned toward the back of the couch, wrapping myself in the blanket and adjusting on his lap. "I hope you didn't sleep sitting up," I said.

"I was comfortable," he said, putting his hand on my side. "I've slept in way worse places than this, believe me. I actually slept really good last night."

"When did you wake up?" I asked.

"A few minutes ago."

"What were you doing," I moaned. "Just being quiet, sitting there?"

"Yep," he said.

I smiled and reached out of the covers so that I could hold his hand. "Thank you," I said once I found it.

CHAPTER 12

⁓

*B*y the time I got my bearings and got off the couch, it was after 9am.

I called my family to wish them a Merry Christmas and let them know I was spending the day with Daniel. I then went upstairs to shower and get dressed. I wore blue jeans and a red sweater. I tied my hair up and put on some black sneakers. I loved dresses and skirts, and I wore them often, but I went with blue jeans because Daniel had already told me that he liked to play backyard football with his cousins, and I wanted the option to get in on that. I wore delicate gold earrings and a lacy, dressy scarf that I had knitted out of some gorgeous maroon yarn. The color blended well with the red of my sweater. I knew I looked Christmas-y but not overdone.

I got dressed quickly, but I tried my best for Daniel. I was upstairs for about thirty minutes before coming back down. Daniel was sitting at the bar, looking at the newspaper with his back to me when I came down. He turned and stood when I came into the room. He had no clothes to change into, so he was wearing the same jeans and t-shirt he had on when I surprised him at the hardware store.

"Hey there, beautiful," he said, smiling at me.

His smile melted me. His voice melted me. Daniel was the thing my heart desired. I had never felt so wholly devoted to a man. I was feeling ooey-gooey just from walking into the same room as him. I walked straight into his arms. I didn't hesitate or stand beside him. I just walked straight up to him and wrapped my arms around his middle, hugging him.

"Hey there, handsome," I said in response to his greeting.

He pulled back to stare at me. "You're beautiful," he said, staring down at me. "I like your scarf and your earrings."

"I made it," I said. "The scarf."

"Crochet?"

"Knit," I said. "I could make you one sometime. A manly one."

He smiled at me for saying that. I reached up and touched his chest, letting my fingertips gently move across the thin layer of cotton t-shirt.

"I'm not going to love on you like this in front of your mom," I said.

"I figured," he answered, causing me to meet his eyes.

"You did?"

He nodded. "I usually don't mention girls to my parents. I've never been the type to talk about that kind of stuff in front of them."

"Is it going to be weird if I go over there?" I asked. "Should I go at all?"

"No, yeah, I want you to come. Obviously, I want you to come. I just, I think you were probably right when you said you wanted to take it easy in front of them."

"Okay, yeah," I said, feeling only slightly heartbroken that he was so easy to convince.

***

I followed Daniel to his house and walked in with him once we arrived. His parents were there, along with his aunt and a few other family members. Everyone welcomed us and wished us a Merry Christmas.

They were a good family. Friendliness came naturally to them, so they were nice and welcoming to me. But there was an edge of quiet curiosity or concern regarding me showing up with Daniel. Nancy asked a few questions about my sister and Billy and their Christmas plans. She asked enough that she got close to figuring out that Daniel and I had been at their house together last night. She relented and stopped questioning any further, changing the subject to apple pie versus pumpkin pie as a favorite dessert.

Daniel went to take a shower and change once he saw that his mom was content talking to me about food. He made sure I would be okay by myself, and I reassured him that I was fine.

"Let me show you something," was one of the first things out of Nancy King's mouth when Daniel left the room. She wiped her hands and motioned for me to follow her.

"Where's Laney?" one of the family members called when we walked through the living room.

"She's coming," Nancy said. "She spent the night with a friend, but she'll be here soon. She's on her way."

I followed Nancy into the office.

"You can have a seat," she said, gesturing to a small couch that lined the wall. "I wanted to show you a letter Daniel wrote a few years back."

It took her a few minutes to find it. We were just quiet while she looked. I was honestly a little scared about what it would say. But she was smiling at me once she found it and brought it over to me, and that eased my mind. I stared down at it. It was written in Daniel's handwriting. I knew it well after I had poured over his letters recently.

Mom and Dad,

I hope everything is good back home. Mother's Day is coming up, and Laney's birthday, so I wanted to let you know that I'm thinking about you both and love you.

I'm doing well over here. I wanted to tell you about something of a miracle that happened to me. I was having a rough night over a buddy of mine who had just passed away, and I remembered something my friend told me. She said if I felt bad I could just open a Bible and start reading, and pretty soon I'd forget what I felt bad about. So, I did that. I opened a Bible to a page at the end of the book of Mark.

I started reading this segment that was titled the great commission. I had heard it before—at least the part about going into the world to preach the gospel. But then I kept reading. And in that same section, it said that we as followers would take up serpents, and that if we drink anything deadly, it would by no means hurt us.

And something in my heart and mind changed when I read that part, Mom. It came across as a promise of safekeeping to me. That verse was God telling me He was going to take care of me. I might be in a situation where I feel like I'm in danger, but ultimately God is in charge of my fate. Nothing's going to kill me before it's supposed to.

This has caused me a great deal of happiness. I now feel brave and not afraid. Don't worry, I'm not going to do anything stupid like jump on a grenade. But I'm also not scared at all. That is something that is valuable over here. It has changed my whole life. I don't know how to put it in words, other than to say that I feel like a new person. I wish I had read that verse months ago. I know that I'm here for a reason. I know I have a job to do. And that verse assured me that I have God's protection and provision in getting that job done.

I will do my very best to get home to you guys and Laney, but know that I am content, unafraid, and trusting in God's plan, no matter what it is.

I love you all. I'll write again soon.
Your son,
Daniel

It took extreme concentration to keep from crying as I read it, but I managed. Barely. I blinked as I folded it and handed it to Nancy.

"I just wanted to thank you," she said.

"Ma'am?" I asked, feeling choked up.

"Thank you, sweetheart. I feel like I owe you so much for that."

"For what?" I asked.

"You were the one who told him to pick up his Bible when he felt scared. I asked him who that friend was who told him that, and he said you had written it in a letter." She shook her head and smiled a little. "You can tell your child something time and time again, but sometimes it takes a friend telling them the same thing for it to sink in. He said you were the one who gave him that suggestion, and I just wanted you to know how thankful I was that you did that. I didn't mention it when I saw you and your sister out to lunch because I didn't have the letter with me, and I didn't know if I could explain it right."

I blinked at her. I did *not* remember telling Daniel that in a letter, but I was happy I had. It gave me a little hope that I wasn't such a bad friend to him after all.

"Oh, goodness, I'm just happy he made it through all that," I said.

"I know," she said as she opened the desk drawer and stashed the letter into it. "Nathaniel said we don't even know the half of what went on over there. One of the other soldiers told a story at the medal ceremony, and I cried all the way home thinking about what Daniel must have gone through. He's always been quiet about the things that happened."

"Gosh," I said, feeling at a loss for words.

But I didn't have to decide what to say because just then, there was noise at the door. The office was near the front entryway, and I turned to face the door when it opened.

"Hey Laney, baby, good morning. Merry Christmas!"

"Merry..." Laney had been in the middle of closing the door when she said that first word, but she turned and laid eyes on me as she said the next word, "Christmas." It didn't come out so friendly-sounding. Her face fell as she stared right at me.

Mrs. King must have been surprised by the response because she let out an uncomfortable chuckle and patted me on the shoulder.

"Abby came to eat lunch with us."

"Oh, okay," Laney said nodding stiffly.

She wasn't being rude enough for her mom to say anything, but she also wasn't acting right. It had been a while since I had seen her, and if I remembered right, that wasn't the most pleasant exchange either. My heart fell at her apparent disapproval, but Nancy acted like she didn't notice it.

"I've got to get back to the kitchen," Nancy said, smiling. "I left your aunt in charge, and I'm not sure if that was such a good idea."

Laney had her hands full, and she had turned to deal with the things she was carrying. A few of them were wrapped presents, and she left them on a bench in the entryway while still holding her other things. Mrs. King had walked off, and Laney was turned the other way, ignoring me, hoping I would walk off with her mom.

"Hey, Laney," I said. I knew I shouldn't have talked to her, but I avoided conflict whenever possible and I simply hated it when someone was mad at me.

"Hey," she said. She turned and started to head into the other room.

"Hey, is something the matter?" I asked, reaching out to touch her arm. She looked at me with a stone-cold expression and pulled her arm away from me.

"Gosh, Laney."

"Gosh, Abby," she said, mocking me, staring at me.

"What's your problem?" I asked.

"You. I don't know why you can't just leave my brother alone."

I flinched. I felt like her words made a physical impact on me. I blinked at her, trying to hold back the instant angry tears that rose to my eyes, stinging. "Thanks a lot," I said, being sarcastic, having nothing else.

"Really, Abby. I can see what's going on here. He spends his whole life waiting for you, and the second he gives up and finds somebody else, you come back to toy with him again. I'm sorry, Abby, I like you as a person. But Daniel's my brother and I love him. I'm protective of him and I'm gonna say something before I sit here and watch him get hurt by you again and again."

I was shocked. I was speechless. I opened my mouth and then closed it again. I was already so torn up about my past choices with Daniel that her words cut me to the core.

"Y-you really knew what you were going to say to me," I said, stunned. "You really just let it fly, just now, didn't you?"

"Well, yeah, Abby. I'm not surprised you're here. I should have known you had something to do with him breaking up with Kelly. He came home from Thanksgiving at Billy's, talking about you being there."

"But, your mom just had me in here *thanking me* for a letter I wrote him."

I was sorry the instant it came out of my mouth. It was a desperate attempt at some sort of redemption, and Laney wasn't buying it, she just kept scowling at me.

"Of course she did," she said. "My mom is *clueless* about my brother. God love her, but she's got her head in the sand when it comes to Daniel and all the crap he's had to go through. She just, her mind can't accept it when any of us goes through something hard. She doesn't even comprehend that he went over there and almost got killed about a hundred different times. She just blocks it out."

My heart felt broken. I didn't know what to say.

Just then, there was a knock on the door. "Knock, knock!" a lady called, opening the door right after she banged on it.

"Hey, Aunt Lisa!" Laney said, acting like a different person. Her face had gone from a disgusted expression to one of bright holiday cheer. "Merry Christmas, y'all!" she said, welcoming her family.

A whole family, mom, dad, and three kids under the age of ten came trampling through the door. They were making so much noise and ruckus that I stepped out of the way to let them through.

"Hello," the lady said to me as they came in.

"Hello," I said, trying to smile at her even though I felt like I might break into a million pieces.

I bowed out of the entryway, headed toward the kitchen. There was a small hallway near the kitchen that led to a door on the side of the house. I hadn't been planning on going out of it. I had been headed to the kitchen where Daniel would come looking for me. But the sight of the great outdoors was too good to pass up.

I felt compelled to make an emergency exit. I felt like if I didn't get some fresh air I might pass out. Suddenly, the air inside was hard to breathe. My heart was racing and my nerves were getting the better of me. I was overwhelmed and doing my best to keep from bawling.

My eyes watered, but I did not let myself cry. I walked out of the door and down the small set of steps leading to the sidewalk. I paced the few feet of grass between the path and the house. I walked three strides one way before turning around and walking the other way. No one was around, so I just paced in circles to get my nervous energy out. I took deep, calming breaths.

I kept having flashes of things Laney said to me. She said her mom's head was in the sand. I saw a visual in my mind of Nancy King bending over with her head down in the sand like an ostrich.

I imagined Daniel hurting.

I thought of Laney knowing I was the one who hurt him.

Daniel almost getting killed.

Laney being mad at me.

Me ignoring Daniel.

Laney knowing that I ignored him.

Thoughts and memories of the different things she said came to me in rapid succession. I felt sick to my stomach at how mad she had been.

I knew and liked Laney. She was a nice girl, and I never would have dreamed she would act that way to someone—especially to me. To say I felt terrible would be putting it mildly. I wanted to crawl under a rock. I, at least, wanted to leave this house.

Yes, leave.

I should and would leave this residence.

I should do it posthaste.

It was my only option.

I patted my pockets, but my keys were in my purse, which was in the house. I had to get them. I took a deep breath as I headed back inside.

CHAPTER 13

Daniel

*D*aniel had felt a lot of emotions in the last five years. He had packed a lot of living into that span of time. He had been places and seen and done things that most people never experienced in their entire lifetimes. He had lived through tragic loss and soaring victories. Out of necessity, he had learned how to control and ultimately suppress his emotions. He was normally practical, level-headed, and not emotional at all.

But then there was Abigail.

She made him feel things that he couldn't suppress—things he didn't want to. She was there to spend Christmas with him and his family, and he was giddy and nervous as a result of it. He left Abby downstairs with his family while he went to his old room to shower and change clothes. He moved quickly, and it only took him fifteen minutes or so.

Daniel put on jeans and a striped sweater that he had worn before and he knew looked good on him. He smiled as he put it on, knowing she would say something about it.

On his way out, he dug in his luggage and came up with a long, slender jewelry box. It contained a necklace he had bought for Abby when he was overseas. It was a beautifully cut rectangular emerald hanging from a delicate gold chain. He had bought it for Abby the week before she told him not to write anymore, and he hung onto it since then.

Even during the time when he thought he wouldn't have her, he wasn't planning on giving the necklace to anyone else. He had bought it for Abby, and it was hers.

He felt child-like excitement that he had it for her for Christmas. He considered taking it downstairs right then, but it was still early, and he had the rest of the day to surprise her with it. He stashed it in his suitcase and headed downstairs to meet her.

More people had arrived at his house since he went upstairs. "Hey, Aunt Lisa," he said, coming into the kitchen.

"Heyyy, you look so handsome, Danny-boy."

"Thank you," he said, giving his aunt a hug. Laney was standing right there, and she reached out and hugged Daniel after Lisa let him go. He patted her on the back and they exchanged Merry Christmases.

"Where's Abby?" he asked, crossing the room, looking toward the living room for her.

His mom was standing at the sink and she gestured behind him. "I think I saw her go out the side door," she said.

Daniel turned and crossed to the hallway that led to the side entrance. He saw Abby through the window, and he smiled at her as he opened the door. She glanced up to look at him the second she heard the door. She smiled, but it was not the same smile she had been wearing earlier. This one was fake.

His heart fell. "What happened?" he said.

"Nothing. I was just coming inside. To get my purse."

There was a small set of steps, and she stood at the bottom of it, looking up at him. Daniel stepped outside, letting the door close behind him. "Come here," he said, gently.

"I thought we weren't doing that in front of your family," she replied, cutting her eyes toward the house as if someone was watching them.

Daniel studied her, knowing something was wrong. "Abby, what's the matter? What happened?"

She took a deep breath, staring up at him from the bottom of the steps. She tried to smile, but it faded quickly.

"Come here," she said quietly, crooking her finger at him.

Daniel instantly took the two steps downward, meeting her where she stood on the path. He tried to take her into his arms, but she stepped back.

"They could be watching," she said. "And I don't want to make a scene or anything, but I think I need to leave. Would it be possible for you to help me get my purse out of the—"

"Make a scene?" he asked, cutting her off. "What are you talking about?"

"I said I don't want to make a scene," she said, as if that clarified anything. She gestured to the house. "I was wondering if it could be possible for you to run into the house and get my purse. It's in the kitchen on that little desk by the lamp."

Daniel positioned his face right in front of Abby's, forcing her to look at him. "What is happening here?" he asked, staring at her, begging her to get back to how she was.

She blinked, staring into his eyes for a few seconds before she took another deep, hopeless breath.

"Listen, Daniel. I just want to leave quietly. It's Christmas, and I don't want to go back in there and give any more attention to this. Your family's here, and I'd really rather just go quietly. Please. Help me do that."

His expression reflected his emotion—confused. "If you're talking about me trying to touch you in front of them, then just… we've talked about that already. I wasn't planning on doing that. I thought we had a plan."

She let out a breath since he didn't understand what was going on at all. Daniel reached out and touched her arm. He tried to pull her into his arms, but she leaned back, gazing up at him.

"Your sister," she said. She cleared her throat. "And she's right, that's why it's so embarrassing. I don't know what I was thinking. I should have known your family would know. I should have known they'd hate me. I feel so stupid."

Daniel continued to stare patiently at her. "Abby, can you start at the beginning? And say it like a hundred times slower than you said it just now. What did my sister say to you?"

Daniel was a no-nonsense, matter-of-fact guy, and he didn't plan on walking back inside until he had a reasonable conversation with her.

She stared at him. Her brown eyes were everything to him. He had taken pleasure in getting lost in them since the first time he looked at her.

She regarded him with a regretful expression. "Your sister is agitated with me, and I can't blame her," she said.

"What did she say to you?" Daniel asked, looking defensive.

"No, no, no, it's not her fault. She was just looking out for you."

"What did she say?" Daniel asked. He took a deep breath. He was shaking with anger, thinking Laney had said something about Kelly. He tried not to let it show.

"She knew you liked me," Abigail said. "She said I should have liked you back all those years, and she was right, Daniel."

"That's all she said?" Daniel asked, looking confused again.

"It's not just that she said it," Abigail said. "She was really mad at me. She doesn't like me. I'm not saying that we need to stop things between us, Daniel, but I—"

"I should hope not."

"But I don't want to go back in there today," Abigail said. "You should just go have a nice Christmas with your family."

He shook his head, wearing a serious expression. "You were trying to leave your sister's house last month when I saw you," he said.

"Yeah," she agreed, not seeing his point.

"Doesn't that seem like a problem to you?"

"What about it?" she asked.

"That you just take off when you get uncomfortable."

"What else would you do?" she asked.

Daniel smiled at her because she actually didn't know. He reached a hand around her waist and pulled her to him. She didn't resist. She stared up at him, waiting to hear what he would say.

"You need to stay and fight sometimes, Abigail."

"I don't want to fight with your sister," she said. "Especially on Christmas."

"You don't have to literally fight. You don't have to get mad and leave, and you don't have to fight with my sister if you stay. There are all sorts of things that can happen instead of those things."

He held onto her. He wanted to keep a hand on her forever, never let her out of his grasp. There was just no way he was letting her leave this house being all flustered like she was—not over something so insignificant.

"Listen, we'll go inside together. I'll tell Laney I need to see her upstairs about a Christmas present. No one will question it. We'll go up and talk for a minute."

"No, see? That's too much. It's too confrontational."

Daniel smiled patiently as he reached up and touched the side of her face. "If we don't talk to her, it'll never get settled, and if it never gets settled, you'll be uncomfortable all day."

"Yes. That's why I was just going to go."

His grin broadened slowly. "Still trying to run away?"

"No," she said. She paused for several seconds. "You're right. I'm sorry. Let's talk to her if you think it'll help."

"It has to help," he said, pulling her inside. "There's no other acceptable option."

Five minutes later, the three of them were in Daniel's old room. Abigail stood on one side, and Laney stood on the other, arms crossed. Daniel closed the door and then came to stand between them.

"Did she tattle on me?" Laney asked.

"Okay, Laney, I don't know what's the matter with you, but we're going to work this out right now," Daniel said. "Actually, it's not anything we need to work out," he corrected. "It's just something we need to establish." Daniel was unapologetic and direct, staring right at his sister. She nodded at him.

He took a deep breath and glanced from one to the other— at two of the women he loved most in all the world. He focused on his sister.

"I'm going to try to put this as plain and in as few words as possible, Laney, and if you don't understand where I'm coming from after that, we can talk more about it, okay?"

She nodded.

"I need you to understand something. The most hurtful, painful thing you could do to me would be to try to keep me and Abby apart. I know you love me and you think you're taking up for me, but listen closely. I. Love. Her."

She let out a scoff.

"Don't," he said resolutely. "Think about what you're doing, Laney, and know that if you hurt Abigail, you hurt me. If you really want to see that I'm the happiest I can be, you'll love her and welcome her, and you'll go down there and eat food and sing carols and whatever else you would normally do. She's one of us, Laney, and if you can't act like it, you'll be hurting me and not helping me."

"Can I just say something?" Abigail asked.

They both looked at her, and she shrank back just a little. She was looking at Laney. "I just want to tell you that you're right. With the way I was in the past, you would be smart to try to get me to stay away from your brother. But I've changed, Laney. I promise I have."

She was sincere and vulnerable, and Daniel went to stand next to her. He pulled her next to him, wrapping his arm protectively around her. Abigail glanced at him with a small, thankful smile before looking at Laney again.

"Even if she didn't change, I don't care. Abby is my girl. Listen to me and hear my words. I'm telling you if you want me to be happy, you'll do whatever you can to keep Abby coming around."

"Forgive me," Abby added, speaking sincerely to Laney. "Please forgive me and let me start over with your brother. I know I didn't deserve him or his loyalty back then, and I might not even now, but I'm… my heart is… I will be good to him."

Laney looked them over, taking in their proximity. "Are you guys supposed to be together or something? Are you going steady with each other now?"

"Yes," Daniel said.

And at the same time Abigail said, "No."

Laney and Daniel both looked at Abigail.

"I was saying that for y'all," she insisted with her hands raised. "So it didn't seem like too much." She looked at Daniel. "You and I talked about not saying anything to your family."

Daniel had one arm on her, but he pulled her closer, demonstrating just how steady they were going. "Yeah, I know we said that, but now that we're already in this situation, I think Laney can see that we're together. I think she probably already gets the idea."

"Yes, then," Abby said, looking at Laney. "We're together. We're definitely together. I'm definitely all in on my end."

Excitement flooded Daniel's body when he heard her say those words out loud. Or maybe it was that she was standing there letting him hold onto her in front of Laney. Either way, he was all stirred-up inside.

"We're together," he agreed.

CHAPTER 14

Abigail

"My brother is just never going to get over you," Laney said, staring straight at me. She crossed her arms in front of her chest and shook her head, looking at me as if she was trying to understand. But her stony countenance had changed. She was being lighthearted, and the sight of it caused me to experience a rush of relief.

"I don't need to get over her," Daniel said.

He broke contact with me and crossed to the area near his bed. He gave his sister a smile and nod, assuming all business had been settled. "You go down first," he said to Laney.

"Mom thinks we're talking about Christmas presents," Laney returned. "What am I supposed to tell her?"

Daniel shook his head. "It doesn't matter. She won't notice. She's got all kinds of stuff going on downstairs."

"Okay, well I guess I'll see y'all down there," Laney said, turning to walk out.

"Is Michael coming?" Daniel asked.

"Yep," Laney called. "He'll be here for lunch."

Michael Elliot was her boyfriend. They'd been together for a couple of years. Michael knew Albert. Michael's dad owned the restaurant where Albert worked. Galveston was small enough that lives intersected like that.

Hearing Michael's name made me think of Albert, and the thought of him made me realize how very in love with Daniel I was. My life would probably look very different if I had still been on that Albert path.

I took in my surroundings in Daniel's old bedroom—the twin bed and sports memorabilia. He hadn't been in there much in the last five years, and he had changed a lot since then. He had traveled all over the world. I was looking around his room feeling nostalgic, thinking about Daniel and his adventures.

He peered in his luggage, and I absentmindedly propped myself onto the foot of the bed, holding onto the wooden bedpost, looking around.

"What's this?" I said when he held a box in the air between us.

"It's a gift," he said.

"For me?"

He smiled but didn't answer. He nudged the box toward me, and I took it from him.

"What's in here?" I asked.

It seemed like a jewelry box. It was the wrong size for a ring, but it looked like a jewelry box for sure.

"Where did you get this?" I asked before I even opened it.

A wide grin spread across Daniel's face. The sight of it made my heart speed up.

"I got it in France," he said.

"You talked about going to France in one of your letters."

"That's when I got it," he said, nodding. "I only went there once. This thing has been everywhere with me."

I wanted to thank him for saving it for me, but the words got stuck in my throat. I swallowed, looking down at the box as I opened it. There was a delicate gold chain, and at the end of it was a gorgeous, shimmering green stone, beautifully cut into a rectangle shape with perfect clarity and sharp facets. It was set on a dainty gold pendant. I took it out of the box, holding the jewel in my fingertips and tilting it this way and that, and smiling at the way the light shone through it.

"Is it for *me*?" I asked.

There had been talk about his mother's Christmas present, so I felt like I should ask.

Daniel let out a little laugh. "Yes, it's for you. Do you like it?"

"I love it so much."

My eyes stung with tears, and I blinked them away as I stared at the necklace. It was classy and elegant. I had never been given something so beautiful, so valuable. I had never been given a real piece of jewelry. I had two jewelry boxes and I liked to accessorize, but everything I owned was inexpensive costume jewelry.

"Is this real?" I asked when that thought crossed my mind.

Daniel reached out and took it from me. He was planning on fastening it for me, and I turned for him and tucked my chin so that he could access the back of my neck.

"Yes, it's real," he said. "I bought it from a store in Paris. It's the one the jeweler recommended specifically for you."

"It's best to listen to the experts," I said. I turned and smiled at him after he got it fastened, touching the place on my chest where it rested. I stepped toward the mirror to take a look at it.

"Did you really tell him who you were buying it for?"

"Yes, I did."

"And you told him it was me?" I asked smiling shyly at him as I looked at myself in the mirror. The small green stone hung at the very edge of my sweater. I turned around so Daniel could see it.

"Yeah, he was right, that looks good on you," Daniel said.

"How would he know what to choose, unless you described me? Did you describe me to him?"

He grinned. "I showed him your picture."

***

"He showed the guy her picture," Laney said, repeating the story later that same day when a few of her friends came over to hang out and play backyard football that afternoon. We were all sitting on the back porch together—eight or ten of us. "He got it in Paris all those years ago, and carried it around, waiting to give it to her." she added, finishing the story.

"And that's what he gave you for Christmas?" Carrie asked.

I nodded and smiled, touching my necklace for the hundredth time that day. Daniel was sitting next to me on the glider, and he reached out and put his hand on my leg in a possessive gesture.

Just as he did that, Michael came outside to join us, and he let out an excited whistle. "We got ourselves a show down, son! A race!"

"Who?" Nick said, getting to the edge of his seat.

"Jimmy Vinson got a new car for Christmas. A Charger. He's gonna take it out on North Taylor Road. Vance and those guys are gonna be out there, racing 'em, man!"

"When?" Nick asked excitedly.

"Sunset."

"That's basically now," Laney said, looking at our surroundings.

"I know," Michael said. He clapped. "Let's go!"

And just like that, our quiet Christmas evening got a little rowdier.

There were three cars of young people who left Daniel's house to go watch some car races.

When I lived here, I had a few friends who drove muscle cars and had talked about going out to North Taylor Road to race, but no one ever really followed through with it. A few years back, there had been a fatal accident, and since then, only hoods or extreme thrill seekers went out there.

There were four of us in Daniel's truck on the way over. Daniel, me, Laney, and then Michael—in that order, squeezed in across the bench seat.

"I'm not sure if I like this," I said, speaking loudly over the sound of the engine and the radio.

Daniel reached out and turned down the music. "Jimmy Vinson's not going to do anything to wreck that Charger," he assured me.

"He's been saving up for that thing since he was a little kid."

Michael laughed. "You're so right. He'd let Vince go on ahead and win if it came down to wrecking that car."

There was a reason North Taylor Road was used for racing. It was wide and flat, and it was so open and deserted that spectators could park on the side of the road and watch the race from start to finish. We all parked next to each other and got out of our cars to watch the action.

Michael and Nick ran over to the starting line to see who all was going to be racing and find out when they planned on getting started. We weren't the only people who had come to watch. There were two other groups of cars parked along the side of the road, all of us sitting on the tailgates of trucks like we were expecting a parade. It was still light out, but the sun was low in the sky. The temperature was cool enough that I adjusted my scarf and crossed my arms in front of my chest to keep warm.

"Come here," Daniel said. He had already found a spot sitting on the edge of his tailgate by the time I made it to the back of the truck. I walked over to him, and he pulled me close, me standing in front of his tailgate and him sitting down on it. My back was to his front, and he was holding onto me so tightly that I was locked into place. It was wonderful.

I didn't care about Jimmy Vinson's new car or about seeing him race it. I would never have dreamed that I would be watching drag racing on North Taylor Road on Christmas night, but there I was. And honestly, it was one of those moments in time that would be locked into my heart forever. Everything about it was amazing—the cool, crisp air, the sunset, the sounds of engines revving and people talking. The ones closer to us were talking, and some in the distance were yelling and getting rowdy. There was excitement in the air, and it wasn't just a result of me standing in Daniel's embrace.

I leaned into his chest, turning and looking up at him. I stretched up and kissed the underside of his jaw, and Carrie saw me. "Aww," she said. "You guys are so romantic. I want to fall in love so bad."

"What are you going to do tomorrow when he has to go back?" Laney asked.

"Don't remind them!" Carrie said, dramatically. "Let them enjoy their beautiful Christmas moment."

"I know, but I'm just wondering what they have planned," Laney said. "Abby's a teacher in Louisiana, and my brother lives in Georgia."

"We haven't talked about it," I said, honestly.

"You haven't *talked about it*?" Carrie said, shocked, dramatic. "Are you *separating* tomorrow?"

"I have to head back," Daniel said, nodding. He was speaking loudly since we were outside and there was noise, and I loved the deep sound of his voice with my ears so close. I leaned into him. "I assume Abby will need to finish the school year. And I'm under contract through the summer, anyway. We'll have to get by with short trips and plan a way to be together this fall. Either she'll come to Georgia with me, or both of us can go somewhere else," he added.

Laney leaned forward, peering at us. "You can't expect me to keep quiet when you're talking about all this in front of me. Of course, I'm going to vote that you to stay here. Come back home."

"I can see us ending up here eventually," Daniel said.

I nodded. "Me too," I agreed, unable to believe we were having this direct conversation in front of everyone.

Jimmy Vinson lost horribly.

He was being so careful with his new car that Vance had an easy victory. None of us really paid attention to the cars. They did a lot of revving and peeling out at the starting line.

Michael, who badly wanted a muscle car, stayed down there with them. The rest of us just sat out there and talked, enjoying the cool temperatures and the beautiful sunset.

We went back to the Kings' house and got into the leftovers after that.

CHAPTER 15

A month later

Somewhere near the Alabama/Georgia state line

*L*eaving Daniel after Christmas was even more difficult than I imagined it would be. I came to figure out that belonging to Daniel and having him belong to me was the most natural thing in the world. It was insanely difficult to part ways with him after Christmas. We did it, but it was not fun.

Both of us went back to work. We called daily, although we couldn't talk as long as we wanted to because of the long-distance charges. We wrote letters, too. Daniel wrote me twice a week like always. I wrote him multiple short notes every day. I included artwork from myself and my students, and stories to go along with them. Most of the notes were nothing fancy— just things I would think of and want to share with him so I would scribble words down on a piece of paper. I saved all my collections and mailed them in a large envelope once a week.

I would see Daniel a month after we parted ways, and between that time, I mailed him hundreds of little notes, thoughts, drawings, etc. Daniel loved getting the envelope every week, and he would call me and we'd laugh about the different things I sent.

Finally, after what seemed like a million years, the last weekend in January arrived. I would soon see Daniel again.

Billy would compete Saturday night in a world championship boxing match. His match was the main event and he would be defending his title. It would be held in Atlanta, Georgia, and filmed and broadcast on national television.

Billy had gotten accustomed to this level of competition, but Tess always got really nervous, which made me nervous. I tried to go to as many of his matches as I could, but this one was a no-brainer since it was so close to Daniel.

I took Thursday and Friday off of work, and ten of us left Texas, headed for Atlanta. Billy and his coaches flew in an airplane, but Tess and the baby traveled with us in the caravan of cars. We left first thing in the morning to make the long journey from Texas to Georgia. It was a fourteen-hour drive by the time we stopped for gas and food.

I called Daniel from a gas station in Alabama. He knew what time we were planning on leaving that morning, so he was waiting for my call that afternoon. He picked up on the first ring. We made plans to meet in two hours on Interstate 85 in a town called West Point, Georgia. Daniel told us a specific interstate exit and filling station where he would be waiting.

***

I saw his truck when we pulled off the road and into the parking lot of the filling station he had described. There were four cars in our caravan, and we all went toward the area on the far side of the station where Daniel's truck was parked.

My mom reminded my dad to buy a city map of Atlanta since the last place didn't have one. I only half-heard her because I was staring at Daniel the whole time we pulled up. He was in his truck at first, but he got out when he saw us.

I had to work to contain my excitement. I almost let out a squeal when he stepped out of the truck and closed the door behind him. He was big, and the sight of his tall, muscular body made me feel giddy in about fifteen different ways.

"Oh, Abigail, there's Daniel!" Mom said casually, as if I didn't already know.

We parked and all got out to stretch our legs. I had been in the backseat of my mother's station wagon, and I was the first one out of the vehicle when we stopped. Daniel and I came toward each other, smiling, both of us with open arms, eager to embrace. My heart was pounding and I was breathless, and I didn't realize either of those things until I was holding onto him. He was solid and he held me tightly.

"Yes ma'am," he said, calling out, answering my mother, I assumed. I hadn't even heard her ask a question. "I'd be happy to make arrangements for you to stay with me, but Fort Benning is just as far from here as Atlanta."

"Exactly," my mom said. "I was just saying that. Your trip home from here is as long as ours to the hotel."

"Yes ma'am." Daniel let go of me just long enough to hug the women who were coming up to him. My mother and his mother were both there, along with Laney and Tess, and little Tara.

"Oh, yeah, don't worry about putting us up. We have nice rooms reserved right there next to the Civic Center," Dad added. He groaned and stretched his shoulders as he walked up to us.

The Galveston crew didn't factor Daniel and me into their hotel plans since I was going to stay with him in Fort Benning. It was currently Thursday evening and Billy's match wasn't until Saturday. That meant I would be spending two nights in Fort Benning before Daniel and I went to Atlanta to watch the match. We could have gone to the hotel in Atlanta with the family and made it a short vacation, but I wanted to see and explore the place Daniel had described to me in phone calls and letters.

We planned this trip weeks ago, and the closer it came to time, the more urgent and impatient both of us became.

Our love was like a campfire, and both of us added wood, and stirred and stoked it. We communicated about important things and we took time to share ideas and make plans. We cared for our relationship, and it thrived.

I felt just how alive it was when Daniel came back to my side after hugging a few of our crew. Seeing him was enough to make me warm and tingly. But having his body right beside me, having him reach out and put an arm around me, it was just heaven. I was out of my mind with happiness and anticipation. I knew what we were about to do, and I was insanely shaken up over it.

"Where's Darren?" I asked, staring up at Daniel as I held onto him.

"He's already over there."

"What about Billy?"

"Billy?" Tess turned around and stared at me when I said that name.

I smiled at her.

"What about Billy?" she asked, wearing a curious expression.

"He's down the street," Daniel said with a little nod.

"Down *this* street?" she asked, looking around with her eyebrows furrowed.

"If I can get everyone's attention for a second," Daniel said, turning and speaking louder since everyone was spread out and murmuring in small groups.

"We would've given you all more notice about this, but Abby and I didn't come up with it until last week, and by that time, we decided to hold out and surprise you." Daniel gestured to his left. "If you don't mind, I'll ask you to take a short detour with me. Just down this street, there's a little church. My buddy, Darren, is an Army chaplain, and he was nice enough to set us up in there and come here with me so that we could—"

"I know you two are not getting married right now, Abigail." My mom interrupted Daniel, and we all looked at her. She was comically grasping at her hair to indicate she wasn't in any shape to attend a wedding.

We all laughed at her because she was obviously joking.

"We actually are getting married right now," Daniel said, reaching out and patting my mom on the shoulder.

"I knew it all day, and I didn't tell a soul," Dad said, grinning proudly and coming to stand by Mom.

"Did you?" Mom asked him with wide eyes.

"*Did he?*" I asked, looking at Daniel as surprised as my mom.

Daniel smiled as he spoke again. "Mr. Cohen did know," he said. "I told him last night. I had to ask him first. Man to man—just to make sure he wasn't blindsided before we did all this." Daniel looked around at everyone. "And, yes, I was okay with blindsiding the rest of you."

They laughed.

"What did my dad say when you called him?" I asked.

"I said *where do I sign*?" Dad said. "I said *welcome to the family.*"

Quentin from the gym let out a whistle, which prompted Michael, Laney's boyfriend, to do the same.

"Wait a minute," Tess said. "Did you say my husband's here? I'm still stuck on that."

"Yes, yes, he is," Daniel said, getting back on track. "Billy's here. He's at the church with Marvin and a few others—some of my friends, from the base, too. They're all over there waiting for y'all. It's less than a mile from here. I'll take you over if you'll follow me. And listen, I know it's been a really long day," Daniel added. "But we're going to take a minute and get married real quick. Abby loves me and I love her. She's coming to stay the weekend with me, and well, the short of it is that the best thing we could possibly do was to get married sooner than later."

"And by sooner, they mean right now," Quentin said.

Everyone laughed.

"Is this really happening?" Tess asked, looking around.

"It is. It's happening," Daniel said. "Everything's all set. Just follow us over there."

***

Within minutes, we were all parked at the enchanted chapel. We took our time getting out of our cars and walking toward the door. It was cold out, but everyone was dressed for it. Daniel and I moved slowly across the small, gravel parking lot and up the path so that we could talk as we walked and let our parents and family digest this decision. Tara was bundled-up, and the crisp evening air felt good to everyone.

The whole group was easy-going about this unexpected detour. They all reacted with excitement. All of them were people we knew and loved, and they all seemed pleased with our decision. There were no questions about whether or not it was the right thing to do. Most of the questions were things like, "Will you finish the school year, or will you quit and move to Georgia?" Tess asked if we were planning on taking a honeymoon, and we laughed because neither of us had even thought of that.

Billy opened the door when we made it closer to the bottom of the steps. "Come on, what's taking y'all so long out here?" he asked.

Tess was beside me and she said, "There's your daddy," in a cooing tone to Tara. The whole moment was gorgeous and surreal. Daniel had invited a few people from the base, and we spent several minutes making introductions and making small talk before Darren took over.

CHAPTER 16

*D*arren was an Army Chaplain, but he was off the clock, and he was wearing slacks and a sweater. A few of Daniel's friends came, but they were all dressed in mostly-civilian clothes also. I told Daniel I would be proud for him to wear his Army uniform, but he said that given the casual nature of our wedding, he would be more comfortable in pants and a nice shirt.

I was happy with that decision once we got there and I took in the whole scene. I had on a simple white cotton dress that my mother had made me in the eleventh grade. It was cold out, and I had on a long coat, so no one really knew what I was wearing underneath.

I took my jacket off and did a quick look in the mirror when we got into the church, but there wasn't a grand bride's entrance or anything. I just came out and met everyone, wearing my simple dress. I found Daniel as soon as I came out, and he smiled at me as I crossed to him. I didn't know if it was because I was wearing white or if he was just feeling that way, but he regarded me with a nostalgic smile that was so warm and genuine, I wanted to melt. I walked over to him, and he took me into his arms.

We made our way to the front of the chapel while everyone else found places in the first few pews. It was a good-sized room, so it looked empty inside with only fifteen or twenty people there.

Daniel decided to leave the lights low in the back of the sanctuary and just turn on some in the front. I loved the way it looked. It was an evening wedding in an old church, and we were all road weary. Everything was dreamlike to me in the most beautiful, perfect way possible.

"Good evening, everyone," Darren said. He smiled. "I have to admit, this is the first wedding ceremony I've ever officiated where you, the guests, did not know you were coming till you got here." Everyone laughed. "I have to say, it's beautiful in here though." He looked around, smiling sincerely. "It's a gorgeous little chapel, and a truly wonderful evening. We're all in the middle of something right now. You're all living your own lives, doing your own things, having your own thoughts. And yet we're all here. We're all using this moment in time to stop and celebrate a life-changing moment in the lives of Daniel and Abigail. This evening, they join their lives in the blessed union of marriage. I know they're excited to be here and to share this time with all of you. I know Daniel personally, and I have talked with him a great deal about Abigail and his feelings and intentions toward her. I have prayed with him about this union. Knowing these things, I see absolutely no reason why these two shouldn't get married. If any of the rest of you have anything negative to say about it, I suppose now would be the time." Darren paused briefly. "And so it is that Daniel and Abigail present themselves to be married today, with their family and closest friends here with them. I know it is their goal to live a life pleasing to God. I know they want to help each other and be each other's biggest fans. They will, no doubt, go through peaks and valleys, but how wonderful it is that they'll be doing it all together." He looked at us. "You two will grow older and wiser together. Congratulations to you both. You'll remember this day as the day you gained a helper in this life, and that is priceless. My wife and I have been married for thirteen years, and I still love her with all my heart. I still can't wait to get home and see her tonight. I hope you two will be able to say that in thirteen years. I think you will." He smiled and focused on the crowd. "Both of them have written some things down in the way of vows, but I believe they're going to save it and share them with each other later. Is that right? Is that what we decided?" Darren looked at us and I nodded at him. "Okay, well, that brings me to the part where I say Daniel, do you come here freely and without reservation to give yourself to Abigail in holy matrimony? If so answer 'I do.'"

"I do."

"Abigail, do you come here freely and without reservation to give yourself to Daniel in holy matrimony? If so, answer 'I do.'"

"I definitely do," I said, excitedly.

This caused everyone to laugh and for Daniel to pull me into his arms. A few people whooped when he did that. Daniel looked at Darren like he could go on with the ceremony even though he was holding onto me. I loved it. I just smiled and hugged him back.

"Okay, Daniel please repeat after me. I, Daniel, take you, Abigail to be my lawfully wedded wife."

Daniel repeated the phrase.

"I will share the rest of my life with you. We will build dreams together. I will offer you support in times of trouble and rejoice with you in times of happiness. I will honor you and cherish you and give you my loyalty for all the days of my life."

He paused between each line so that Daniel could repeat the words, and then he did the same for me.

We exchanged rings after that. Darren said a few simple things about them and their symbolism. Daniel had a ring he bought me in Georgia. I had been busy with getting my classroom set up for the substitute teacher, but I drove to Lake Charles to buy him a band last week.

"I pray that your life together is blessed with good health and prosperity," Darren said. "I pray that you have open and honest communication. I pray that you always respect each other's individual talents and gifts and give each other full support in your professional and personal pursuits. May you create a beautiful home and life together. May all the years to come be filled with celebrations and moments to renew your love. May your marriage be filled with respect, loyalty, contentment, affection, and devotion." He took a deep breath and smiled. "And now, by the power vested in me by the State of Georgia and the United States Army, it is my great honor and delight to declare you husband and wife. You, Daniel, may finally ki—"

He just stopped talking and everyone clapped and yelled because Daniel was already kissing me.

He was insatiable. He took a hold of me with a firm grip. He kissed me lightly at first and then he pulled me closer and kissed me hard. He held me tightly around the waist, pulled me in, and kissed me like he meant it. It was the first time we had laid eyes on each other in a month, and there had been a lot of anticipation while we were apart. Especially in the last week—once we decided we were getting married.

Everyone was so excited about the impromptu wedding, that we stayed in the church and visited for a little while even though we all still had driving to do. Darren knew of a restaurant nearby, and he drove to it and picked up chicken and biscuits so that we could enjoy a meal together before getting back on the road. It was quick and easy and really delicious, and we sat around in the back of the chapel eating bites of honey-covered chicken on the best biscuits I had ever tasted.

I was so excited and distracted, however, that I only took a few bites of the meal. I wasn't hungry. I took a small portion of food, but I was talking so much that I just held it on the napkin and barely ate it. Daniel must've taken note that I wasn't eating because he held a piece of honey-coated fried chicken up for me to taste. I was not hungry, but I wasn't about to turn down eating out of his hand. I held his hand steady, guiding it to my mouth. I wasn't obvious with everyone around, but I took it from him slightly slower than necessary and I also accidentally put a little bit of his finger into my mouth when I took the bite. Daniel's other hand was resting on my leg, and I felt his grip tighten, which made me smile.

Once we finished eating, everyone decided it was time to get back on the road. We were giving goodbye hugs when Billy said, "Tomorrow night, we've all been invited to share dinner and a party with Teddy Thomas. He said I should bring anyone who wanted to go. He lives in Atlanta, so it's at his home. But it'll be big—live music and lots of people and everything."

"No kidding!" Quentin said, looking excited.

Teddy Thomas was a famous boxing promoter. I knew he was the one behind this event but I never thought we'd all be invited to go to his house. Daniel and I were planning on staying in Fort Benning until Saturday when we drove up for the match, but I smiled at him when Billy mentioned the party.

"Maybe we could head to Atlanta a day early," I said.

He nodded easily. "I'll call tomorrow morning and see if there's any room in that hotel everyone else is staying in."

"Don't be silly," my mom said. "Even if there's no room, we'll just put you in with one of us. We'll make room."

"That'll be fun," I said, raising my eyebrows at Daniel. "Are you sure it's okay if we all go to that party?" I asked Billy.

"Yeah," Billy said. "Even you guys," he added, gesturing to Daniel's Army friends. "I wouldn't have mentioned it if I wasn't inviting everyone. Teddy told me I could bring as many guests as I wanted."

"I'd be happy to go," Darren said.

"Me too," James, one of the other Army guys, added.

Laney's boyfriend had been talking to the soldiers since we got there, and he gave James, who was standing next to him, an excited pat on the back when we figured out we'd all be seeing each other again the following night.

And that was that.

I came into that tiny Georgia town single, and I left as a married woman—one with plans to go to big parties in big cities.

CHAPTER 17

*O*ne caravan took off for Atlanta, but I was with the ones headed to Fort Benning. Daniel and Darren both drove their trucks, and the other guys had hitched rides with them.

James was willing to squeeze into Darren's truck so that Daniel and I could ride back alone, but I assured them I was fine with having James ride with us. I wasn't just doing that to be nice. I was easy-going with that sort of thing, and it also gave me an excuse to sit even closer to Daniel while he was driving.

We had the same seating arrangement the following afternoon when we all made the trip to Atlanta. The exact same four guys who went to the wedding also went to Atlanta with us the following day. Daniel and I got a room near the Civic Center, in the hotel with everyone from Texas.

James had an aunt in Atlanta, so he and the other Army guys made plans to stay the night with her. Billy had secured their tickets to the match, so they would also be going with us to that the following night.

I didn't understand how much Billy loved and respected Daniel until recently. I knew they were close, but their relationship was deeper than I even realized, and that was a sweet, unexpected bonus. Billy looked out for Daniel's friends, getting them tickets and making sure they were invited to the party. It made me feel proud of both Daniel and Billy, which put me in a happy sort of settled, reflective mood.

I sat in the front seat of Daniel's truck, sandwiched between Daniel and James, on our way to Atlanta. It had rained some early in the trip, so some of our bags were in the front with us. We were crammed in there, and I loved every second of it.

Billy gave Daniel directions that took us right to the hotel. We stayed there for a few hours before getting dressed to go to Teddy's party. I brought a couple of nice outfits with me so that I would have options once I got to Atlanta. I went with a red skirt with matching tights and a blouse that was mostly white with some pink and red.

Billy and Michael came to our room to hang out while all the guys were there. It was a small room, and they were sitting around, cutting up and looking handsome.

In years past, I would have killed to be in that room. It was teeming with good-looking, hard-bodied, well-bred, good-hygiene-having, young gentlemen. There were athletes and soldiers, seven of them in my small hotel room. Years ago, I would have fought tooth and nail to be in a room like that.

But not anymore. I belonged to the best one of the bunch, and I only had eyes for him. It was pretty much a miracle how uninterested I was in other men. I had no desire to so much as look at anyone else.

I left the guys in the room while I went to Tess and Billy's room to finish my routine and help her get ready. We were in there for about a half-hour while we finished getting dressed, and then she fed Tara before we left.

It was the first time she and I had the chance to catch up privately since the day before, and she asked me some sisterly questions about our wedding night. She could see how very in love I was, and the whole conversation was full of loaded questions and giggling. We had heart-to-hearts all the time, but we always respected each other's privacy and didn't ask questions that were too personal. That being said, there was still a fair amount of blushing during that conversation.

Tess and Billy had an adjoining room with our parents, and Mom would be babysitting while Tess and Billy went to the party. Tess made sure Mom had Teddy's phone number in case they needed to get in touch, and she also promised they wouldn't be too long. Mom assured her that Tara would sleep and be fine and that we should take our time.

We went down the hall to my room where the guys were waiting. James had a deck of cards and he was dealing blackjack, using the king-size bed as a table with all the guys standing and sitting around, playing hands.

He turned over a card, and they all yelled at once. They were being rowdy, and it made my heart race. I watched Daniel interact with them. It was a boys-will-be-boys situation with all of them spread out in the room. And Daniel was the one who linked them all together. They were laughing and enjoying each other's company, and the sight of it translated to me feeling proud of him.

I was wearing the necklace he gave me with some dangly earrings. Tess and I were both excited about the evening out, and we dolled ourselves up like the good old days when we shared that apartment.

Daniel made eye contact with me during the commotion of the blackjack game, and I smiled shyly at him. That was enough. He tossed his cards onto the bed.

"I lost, anyway," he said easily. "And we gotta go."

He was walking toward me as he said it. I was by the door, and he came to me, looking hungry, looking predatory. You would think I hadn't seen him in days with how he was staring at me.

And that was how it went for the next two hours. Daniel had a hand on me constantly while we were at the party. And when he didn't, he made sure to come back quickly.

Yesterday was our wedding day.

Last night was our wedding night.

Everything was still so new.

We had gotten to know each other in a new special way last night, but there was still so much to learn. Daniel was everything I could want in a man. He was full of wonderful contradictions. He was innocent yet confident, masculine yet gentle and considerate.

We moved around at Teddy's house, talking to different groups of people and checking out different rooms. It was cold out, so the party was all indoors, but it was a mansion, and most of it was open to guests. There were a lot of people at the party. I had honestly never been to anything like it, and I was thankful and happy to have Daniel next to me, my strong, stable man.

His hands found me in some way or another all evening. Sometimes, it was up by my shoulder or arm, and sometimes, he would hold onto my waist or touch my leg. He touched me constantly. The way his hands roamed discreetly but confidently, with husbandly familiarity, made me feel all kinds of bodily sensations.

He was talking to a couple of guys to his left, but his right hand was on me, and I held it in place, loving my place in the room, loving how I was able to people watch and be quiet or get in on the conversation around me when I wanted.

"We're going back to the hotel," Tess said, leaning over to speak to me over the loud music that was playing in the living room.

This was the same room where the live band had been playing earlier, but they were taking a break, so pre-recorded music was being pumped out of the speakers. The whole house must've been connected to the same speaker system because whatever was playing in this room was also playing in other rooms of the house. It was basically loud everywhere.

"It's only eight-thirty," I said, leaning in to speak to her.

"I know, but Billy's got to get back to get ready for tomorrow, and I want to get back to Tara, anyway. Marvin's riding with us. He was ready to leave an hour ago."

"Should we go, too?" I asked. It was fun there, but I didn't mind the idea of leaving.

"No, no, no," Tess said, shaking her head. "Billy already told Teddy we were leaving, and he made sure to say he wanted you guys to stay."

"I think they're about to play some cards," Daniel said, leaning toward us when he heard what Tess said. "James said Teddy has a table in the basement and he wanted him to set up a game down there."

"All right, then, y'all have it worked out," Tess said. She hugged me. "Love you, sister. Have fun."

"Thank you, love you," I said.

She stepped toward Daniel. "Do you know how to get back to the hotel?" she asked.

"Oh, yeah, that's no problem," he said.

They hugged each other.

We spent another few seconds saying goodbye to Billy and Marvin, and then the three of them took off.

We stayed there for another hour, talking, meeting new people, and listening to music. Teddy came up to our group a little while after they left. He had a huge personality, and he stopped to talk to each of us, like a politician.

"James, James, Sergeant James from Ohio. That's my card-dealin' man right here," he said, nodding and shaking James's hand. "We gonna get you a game set up down there in the basement in a little while, my brother. My boys Chester and Big Lou over there both wanna get in on that."

"Yes sir," James said, "I'll deal anytime you're ready."

"All right, how about you? Who do we have here?"

"I'm Darren Rutledge."

"Sergeant?"

"General, technically, but I go by Chaplain."

"Chaplain, huh?" Teddy bowed and made the gesture that was the sign of the cross. "Bless you," Teddy said.

"Bless you, too," Darren returned easily with a smile and nod.

"Welcome to my home. I hope y'all have been finding everything you need here."

I wasn't really paying attention to the conversation that was happening around me. I heard them talking, but I was mostly concentrating on Daniel's fingers, which had been roaming gently over the small of my back.

I looked back at him when he stopped moving, but he was lost in thought.

"I'm Michael Elliot," Michael said, speaking loudly over the rock song that was playing.

He and Laney had come to stand right beside us, so Teddy stepped our way, basically standing right in front of me.

"Are you from Texas, Michael?"

"Yes, sir."

"So, you're not *Sergeant or General*?"

"No, sir. I'm in the restaurant business."

"All right, all right, that's pretty good. What kind of restaurant?"

"Seafood, sir. Since we're right there on the water."

"Are you successful, Michael."

"Yes, sir."

Teddy smiled. "I'll have to get with Michael later, too. I've been wanting to get in the restaurant business."

Daniel stayed still. I wondered if he had gotten nervous, thinking that we would be next in line to talk to Teddy. But I knew that wasn't the case. Daniel had been talking to people all night. He was a well-spoken, friendly guy. I had even seen him talking to Teddy earlier.

Michael continued saying something about his father's restaurant, but I turned and focused my attention on Daniel. The first thing I noticed was that little muscle flexing at his temple and in front of his ear as he gritted his teeth. He was staring into space, which was not like him at all.

"Daniel," I said his name softly and waited, but he didn't respond.

I thought I could see sweat forming on his face, and my heart pounded. They were still talking beside us, but I couldn't hear them. All I saw was Daniel, and all I heard was the rock rhythm of the song and the lyrics

The drummer relaxes,
and waits between shows,
for his cinnamon girl.

"I have to go," Daniel said stiffly.

"That's my brother and his wife." I heard Laney say it only because she patted me on the back.

"I met Daniel." Teddy said. He laughed. "Though I didn't know he was an American hero when I met him. I heard you earned the Congressional Medal, my brother. You didn't tell me that when we—"

Teddy stopped talking abruptly when I stood between him and my husband, smiling sheepishly.

CHAPTER 18

"*I*'m so sorry, but I just remembered I left my glasses, and my pocketbook—*all* of my, personal items in your ladies' room just now. Oh my goodness. So sorry you guys, we'll be right back."

I acted just flustered and overwhelmed enough that everyone's attention was on me. They were all looking at me and not Daniel as I turned and scrambled away, pulling Daniel with me. I had him tightly by the hand, and I blazed a trail through crowds of people.

I had gone this way to use the restroom earlier. There were a few bathrooms around, and most of them were closer, but I went directly to the one I had found earlier. It was on the other side of the kitchen. I knew you couldn't hear the music from in there. I had noticed it earlier because one of my favorite songs was playing and I was sad when I went inside and couldn't hear it.

I headed straight for that bathroom because, somehow, in the middle of all that commotion with Teddy, it registered that

Daniel needed to leave because of the song that was playing. I was almost sure I was right about it because he had stopped moving right when it came on.

I could still hear it playing as I headed to the small half-bath on the far side of Teddy's kitchen. No one was around. I went straight into the bathroom and pulled Daniel in with me.

It was so small that I leaned against the lavatory to make room for him to come in. I tugged him inside and then I closed and locked the door behind us. It was quiet in there, but I flipped the switch that turned on the vent, making sure to drown out any remnants of the song.

Daniel took a long, deep breath.

He was standing in the only open space in the bathroom. It was so packed in there that I sprang up and sat on the edge of the sink to make room for him. The counter was sturdy and could easily hold my weight. It made me a couple of inches taller to sit there, which put me closer to Daniel. I pulled him in and my eyes met his. His eyes had been watering, and they were still shiny from it. He stared at me.

"I'm so sorry," he whispered stiffly.

I pulled him in, wrapping my legs and my arms around him, locking him in, like I was a koala.

"Why in the world would you be sorry?" I asked, snuggling him. "I was scared of talking to Teddy, anyway. I was wanting to run off."

"Why would you be scared of talking to Teddy?" he asked.

I shrugged. "I don't know. He was talking to all of you guys about your awards and playing cards and everything, and I'm just a teacher."

I loved being a teacher. This whole conversation was a diversion. And it seemed to be working. Daniel's breathing had slowed considerably. I sat there and hugged him. And then, out of nowhere, I sang.

Hello, I love you,
Won't you tell me your name?
Hello, I love you,
Let me jump in your game.

I wasn't a terrible singer, but I was impersonating Jim Morrison and being a little dramatic and silly. Also, I was trying to get another song in his head.

"You better not be singing any Doors songs," he said dryly.

"Why not?' I asked, wondering if they had an effect on him also.

"Because you used to have a big crush on Jim Morrison."

"Jim Morrison has nothing on my husband," I said with certainty.

"Well, I *am* still alive," Daniel said. "I've got that going for me."

"Yes, you are," I said. "You're very much alive."

I pulled back to look at him. He was somehow still the boy I remembered meeting years ago and also the most masculine, handsome man I had ever seen. And he was my one and only. I wanted to care for him. I wanted to help him.

There were several washcloths stacked in a neat pyramid near the sink, and I reached over and picked up the one off the top. I turned to get some cold water on it. Daniel had sweat on his forehead, and I ran the folded, damp washcloth over it. He closed his eyes, and I carefully wiped his handsome face.

"Was it the song?" I asked.

He was still for a second, but then he nodded with his eyes closed. I finished wiping and stashed the damp washcloth on the edge of the counter. I blew gently on his face. I wasn't really the blow-on-a-guy's-face type, but it seemed like a good time to do it. The corner of his mouth rose just enough that I knew he enjoyed it.

"You smell like lemonade."

"I just drank lemonade," I said. "I taste like lemonade, too," I added.

My legs were still wrapped loosely around him, and I flexed them when I said it.

Daniel opened his eyes. He took a deep breath in and then let it out, all while staring at me. I had no idea what he was thinking. "When I first came in here, I thought I might lose it, Abby. I thought I might explode or, at the very least, get sick. But not, now." He took a deep, cleansing breath. His expression was serious and his eyes roamed over my face slowly.

I bit the inside of my bottom lip as I stared up at him. "What do you feel like now?" I asked.

My heart raced as I waited for his answer. He had been touching me lightly all night—touching me discreetly but in ways that made me know he wanted to be with me alone.

"Now, I'm just feeling like being next to you," he said simply. He leaned closer to me crowding my space.

I took an uneven breath, staring at him. There was not room for the both of us in this bathroom, and I absolutely loved being crammed against the vanity with Daniel leaning into me. His big, hulking form was so imposing that I was breathless.

"I want you next to me," I said, being gentle with him.

"Thank you," he said.

I blinked up at him. He came closer. Our faces were only inches apart now.

"Thank me?" I whispered, innocently. "Thank me for winding up in here like this? Why, you're welcome, Daniel. It's entirely my pleasure." I let my outstretched fingertips roam gently over his back and sides.

I pulled him closer with my arms and legs, and that was it. Daniel ravished me. He kissed me in a way I had never been kissed before. Our mouths opened, and Daniel kissed me hard. He did it so wholeheartedly that it was almost as if he wanted to create enough passion and emotion to overwhelm and overcome the other, unwanted emotions.

He pressed against me, holding the back of my head, gripping my hair. For a few seconds there, Daniel wasn't so gentle. He wasn't hurting me, it felt amazing, honestly, but he was more physical than he had been. He had some adrenaline to get out, and I was a willing participant in helping him with that. He asked for full control, and I gave it to him, doing my best to react in ways that let him know I wanted to be his everything. I wanted to be the one to stand beside him and be prim and proper when needed, but I also wanted to be the one he could take into the cramped bathroom and kiss senseless if he needed to.

We were in that tiny bathroom for way longer than it took for the song to end. By the time Daniel finished what he needed to do in there, my mouth was pink and swollen. We laughed at ourselves, and ended up taking a minute and using that cool, damp washcloth to get ourselves in order before we went back out there. I even powered my nose.

Daniel kissed me several more times during all of this resituating, but they were all playful and extremely gentle. I moaned when he finally pulled back far enough for me to hop down off of the edge of the sink. He smiled and leaned in to give me one last quick kiss. I wanted to stay in there forever and never go back out to the party, but Daniel took a hold of the door handle after he broke that last kiss.

"Okay my baby, I guess we have to go back out there," he said before he opened the door.

"You're my baby, too," I said, hopping to my feet.

"I know I am," he said. "Don't you forget it."

"I won't," I said, widening my eyes at him, flirting with him.

Daniel gave me a challenging expression. "I'll just put you in the car and take you back to the hotel if you want to look at me like that."

"I would go back to that hotel with you in a split-second," I said.

His eyes widened as he nodded. "Let's go."

"You guys already said you're playing cards," I said. "We can go back later."

"I didn't say I was playing any cards," Daniel said. "I don't care about that. James and them can stay all night if they want. The others will be fine, too. Michael's got Laney. I'm not worried about them."

"We have already been here a few hours," I said.

"So, are you taking me back to the hotel?" he asked, staring at me.

I grinned and nodded. "I was staying for you."

He shrugged. "If it's up to me, then, let's go."

The next thing I knew, Daniel opened the door, and headed out of the bathroom. He pulled me behind him in much the same way I had pulled him toward the bathroom a few moments earlier. We went through rooms with crowds of people until we reached the place where most of our group was standing.

Laney was standing near the edge of the group, and so was James. Music was playing loudly, a groovy Bill Withers song I recognized.

"Abby and I are taking off," was the very first thing out of Daniel's mouth.

"Is everything okay?" Laney asked, shooting me a concerned expression.

"Yeah, we're just ready to get back," Daniel said. "Does anyone want to ride with us?"

"We drove," Laney said. "But you might want to ask Quentin and Barb. They rode with us."

Daniel looked into the living room where Quentin and his girlfriend were dancing in a group of people. "I think they're fine," he said. "I'm taking my wife back to the hotel."

"Oh, is that what this is about?" Laney asked, almost seeming relieved.

"Yeah," Daniel said, not being shy at all. "It's been fun," he said, hugging his sister. "Y'all have fun and be safe tonight," he added, giving James a pat on the shoulder.

We said goodbye to a few others on our way out, but within minutes, we had found our way to his truck. I sat right next to him even though there was no one else in the truck with us.

CHAPTER 19

Daniel

The following evening

Blue corner locker room

*B*illy was in the zone. The title was his to defend. It was just another day at the office—at least that was what Dizzy kept saying. Daniel was in the locker room with Billy, Dizzy, and Marvin as they warmed up and got ready for the match.

Billy made conversation with all of them while Dizzy wrapped his hands. That was how it was in the locker room. Billy set the tone. Sometimes they were quiet, and sometimes they spoke, but it was never rowdy and the conversation in the room was always slow and easy, like his name.

Easy Billy Castro.

It was embroidered on the back of the shirt Daniel was wearing. He, along with Marvin and Dizzy would be in Billy's corner tonight. It was an honor for Daniel to be in his friend's corner. Billy was the two-time world welterweight champion, and tonight he was looking to defend his title again.

Daniel hadn't been around to go to many of the fights that led Billy to this point. But the two were good friends, and they had kept in touch and encouraged each other through the years.

It had been a long time since Daniel trained regularly at a boxing gym, but he was big and strong enough that his stature and past experience made him a good training partner for Billy.

He was invited to the locker room so that he could hold pads during Billy's pre-match workout. Dizzy was delighted to pass that responsibility to Daniel for the night, and he said more than once that Daniel should just be part of the fight team from then on. It was yet another thing that made Daniel feel like he wasn't going to reenlist this summer.

Abby was open to it, but he knew that if he stayed in the military, he would have to ask for a transfer. He ran into Kelly on a fairly regular basis and he saw her father all the time. He managed to keep it professional, but things hadn't been quite the same since the breakup. That was understandable, though. Love was known for making things messy.

Kelly had fallen head over heels for Daniel, and she made it clear that she still had feelings if he ever wanted to come back to her. She didn't cross any lines, but Daniel knew better than to make a home in Fort Benning with Abby. If moving wasn't an option, or Daniel had family there, he might feel differently. But as it stood, he had no ties to Fort Benning and he thought it was best for them to move on in the fall. He was thinking about that while they were in the locker room.

"Quentin stayed at Teddy's till two o'clock in the morning," Dizzy said, drawing Daniel from his thoughts.

"James and them stayed late, too," Daniel added.

"Quentin said Frank Wells was there," Billy added.

(Frank Wells was Billy's opponent tonight.)

"I wasn't going to say anything about that," Daniel said. "But that's what I heard, too."

"I *told* Billy he was gonna show up there last night," Marvin said. "That's why we left early. I bet Teddy set that up so he could get photos of them exchanging words."

"I was doing good staying out as long as I did," Billy said. "I've got a baby. I'm on a strict schedule."

"It's better than staying out," Marvin said. "You can't do that the night before a match."

"I heard he was there till after midnight," Dizzy said.

"That's why he's getting ready to lose," Marvin added.

"How does it feel to be a married man?" Billy asked, glancing at Daniel with a mischievous grin. "I remember us eating lunch on that very first day. I was trying to take Tess out, and you two tagged along. You were telling her jokes, trying to impress her, your voice cracking all over the place."

"My voice was not cracking." Daniel insisted, smiling.

Billy laughed. "It wasn't *settled*, I'll tell you that. *Gee-golly, Abigail, should we go with them to lunch?*" Billy imitated Daniel's voice, but made it crack.

Daniel was easy-going and confident enough to laugh about it. He also knew it was pretty much the truth.

Daniel's mind raced with hopeful thoughts of how capable and prepared Billy was. The truth was, he was nervous. He had been to a few of Billy's fights, but he had never been in his corner. He felt a certain level of responsibility or pressure with that.

Someone came in and gave them a warning when there was only one minute until walk-out.

Marvin moved to stand in front of Billy at that point. "Listen, Billy. Some men paint pictures, some men write books. Some men make music, and others build houses and cars. But some of us, Billy, some of us were just created to be warriors. For some of us, our bones want to fight other bones. We were built for it. That's just how it is."

Daniel thought of his mom who had cried when she heard that he and his dad were going to take lessons at a boxing gym. Now that she knew these athletes personally and what a passion they had for the sport, she felt differently. She was in the audience at this very moment.

So was Abigail. Daniel smiled at the thought.

But he snapped to when Marvin, still giving the pre-match speech, reached out patted Billy's shoulders with two hearty pats.

"You were created for this, Billy. That's why it's easy for you. That's why I gave you that name. Easy. Now let's win this match, so we can go home and get back to work, you understand?"

"Yes sir."

"You're number one, son. That belt is right where it belongs. Just go out there and show 'em whatcha got. Let's have fun. (More patting.) Show 'em how you work, all right? Show 'em what you were born to do."

"Yes sir."

The guy at the door peeked his head into the room. "Blue Corner, Billy Castro. We're ready for you."

The next thirty minutes were amazing for Daniel. He had seen and done a lot of incredible things in his life, but this experience was right up there with the best of them.

He was with Marvin and Dizzy as they followed Billy to the ring. There were more than ten thousand people in the crowd, and they loved Billy. It was loud and chaotic.

Daniel was so desensitized to chaos that he was able to relax and take it in. He had a good time watching people look at Billy as he walked up. He liked seeing their reactions. Daniel had already scoped out the location where the Galveston group was sitting.

His eyes found Abigail's as soon as he was close enough to see her amongst the people and glare from the light. This woman had managed to mesmerize Daniel for years. She was sitting next to her sister in the crowd, and he could still see them as the girls sitting across the booth at Carson's Diner. Now that they were married and thinking about moving back to Galveston, he was sure he'd be seeing them in booths at Carson's diner for the rest of his life. That thought made Daniel smile absentmindedly, but it was fleeting because the noise and chaos of the boxing match was ongoing.

He stood next to the ring on ground-level while Dizzy and Marvin climbed the steps and went into the ring with Billy to do their coaches' routine. Marvin was talking to Billy while Dizzy checked his gloves, shorts, and shoes.

In addition to warming Billy up in the locker room, Daniel had been given the duty of being Billy's cutman. He had some emergency medical training from the Army, so it was a given that Marvin would ask him to do it rather than having the boxing commissioner provide one like they normally did. In the event that Billy would get a cut, Daniel was the guy prepared with supplies to tend to it on the spot. He was fully capable of it, but he had never done anything like this, at least not in front of thousands of people. He enjoyed the thrill of it all.

He glanced at Abigail again. Her sister was on her right, but his friend, James, was the person on her left. She and James were talking to each other when he looked that way.

He had spent so many years being jealous of the guys Abby was talking to that it was his first instinct to feel that way. But then he remembered she was his. She married him and she had given herself to him in vulnerable ways.

He trusted her, and instead of being jealous, he was happy that she got along so well with his friends. He had all of those thoughts in the span of just a couple of seconds as he glanced at her in the audience.

She happened to look his way before he glanced away, and her face instantly broke into a huge grin. She touched her hands to her mouth and blew him a dramatic kiss with both hands. "I love you," she said. He couldn't hear her, obviously, but he could read her lips easily.

Daniel's smile broadened and he gave her a nudge of the chin. Abigail was more than satisfied with that reaction. She didn't expect him to react any other way since he was in front of thousands of people.

Daniel had a casual response, but there was a feeling of warmth in his chest. Abigail was in love with him. He could see it. It gave him a certain level of peace in a moment of anticipation, excitement, noise, and battle. He turned his attention to the ring.

Fighting was an art to Billy.

Daniel admired that about him. It was something he tried to emulate as a soldier. Billy loved his profession, and he spent time and energy honing and perfecting his skills. That was obvious when he stepped into the ring and started working.

The match went four rounds, and Billy came out with the victory. It was a pleasure and honor to be ringside with the team. There was nothing like watching a sport at its highest level. The skill, technique, and stamina were beautiful to behold, and it was a privilege to be a part of the celebration afterward.

CHAPTER 20

Abigail

Four months later

*I*t was a beautiful afternoon in late May, and I had just finished my last school year in Louisiana.

I had already told my principal I wasn't coming back next year, so I was officially finished working for the Calcasieu Parish school system.

I was currently visiting Galveston for a few days, but I had plans to move in the upcoming weeks in order to prepare for Daniel's arrival in September. I had come on this trip to look at a house for us to buy.

I was sitting at a restaurant table with my sister and Laney King. It was the restaurant Laney's boyfriend's family owned, and we met there for lunch before we went to look at the house.

"I can't believe you're moving back," Laney said.

"I know," Tess agreed. "It doesn't seem real."

"I still don't feel like I'm even done with the school year," I said. "While I was waking up every day, going through the motions, doing my routine, it seemed like it was taking forever. But here we are. I'm finished, and I'm in Galveston."

"Not to stay yet, though," Laney said.

"No, but that'll be happening soon."

Laney reached out and shook my leg under the table. "Thank you for bringing my brother back," she said. "He was convinced you'd want to spend a couple of years at Fort Bragg or even somewhere overseas."

"He offered, but I thought, I don't know, running a hardware store is way safer than being in the Army. You know, if he'd ever get called back over there or anything. Plus, we can just go on vacations if I ever want to see Germany, Japan, or Fort Bragg."

Laney laughed, obviously delighted for her big brother to be coming home.

"Whose house is this again?" Tess asked.

"Evelyn's uncle," I said. "She knew we were going to be moving here this summer, and she called and told me about it last week. It's not on the market or anything. We'd just be buying it directly from him—with a lawyer or whoever does the paperwork. I'm trying not to get my hopes up, but it'd be cool if it worked out."

"Where is it?"

"It's on 20th and Avenue M. I had no idea what it looked like until a couple of minutes ago. I drove by it on the way here.

I've actually seen it and noticed it before. It's shady and tucked back on a little lot. It's got a picket fence and a porch that goes all the way across the front. It's waaaaay better than I expected for the price she mentioned. If Daniel thinks we can afford it, I'm telling Evelyn we want it."

"You haven't even seen the inside," Laney said.

I shrugged. "At this point, with how much I love the outside, I'd be willing to forgive a lot on the inside. Evelyn said it was nice, though."

My sister and my sister-in-law clapped, squealed, and celebrated.

"I have to use the restroom," Laney said, looking around after that. "If Shannon comes back, please tell her I'll have the grilled fish sandwich and some more ginger ale."

She had only been gone a few minutes when Albert, my ex, walked up to our table. He used to work at this restaurant, but he was there as a customer today. He was with another guy, Tommy, who I recognized. Tommy hung back at their table, which was close to the door.

"How are you?" Albert asked, smiling and being charming, looking smooth, looking like Jim Morrison with his long, surfer haircut.

In the past, I would have fallen for it all over again, but this time, I was completely neutral toward him. I felt no attraction whatsoever.

"Hey, Albert," I said.

"What are you doing on my island, Abby Road?" He reached in to hug me, and I stretched up, giving him an awkward one-armed side hug.

"It's her island now," Tess said.

Albert stared at me. "Are you moving back?"

"Yes," I said.

He made an excited expression. "Right on, man. We'll have to get together. What's going on? Did you take a teaching job here?"

I cleared my throat. "I got married," I said.

Albert let out a laugh. "What? You're *married?* Are you serious? To who?" He was so dumbfounded and amused that I shot him an offended stare. "You're just still... so young," he said, backpedaling and looking at me like I was the last person he ever expected to see married.

"What are you doing here, Albert?" Laney asked from several feet away as she came up to our table. She was moving quickly, and she walked in front of him, pushing him aside, forcing him to take a step back. Her question was straightforward, her tone unfriendly.

"I'm having lunch," he said. "Hello to you, too, Laney King."

"I wasn't asking what you were doing at the restaurant. I was asking what you're doing at this table. My brother would not appreciate you being over here talking to Abigail. He'd kick your *rear end* if he saw you over here right now." She stared at Albert, daring him to stay at our table.

He nodded thoughtfully, his expression reflecting his new understanding of the situation. "You married Daniel King?" Albert asked, looking at me.

"Yes," I said.

But Laney spoke louder than me. "Yes, so show some respect," she said. "My brother would not be happy if he saw you in here talking to Abby."

Albert turned and looked over his shoulder as if it dawned on him for the first time that Daniel could be there.

"Good to see you, Albert," Tess said, chiming in trying to put an end to his visit.

"Yeah, y'all too," he said. "I gotta split, anyways."

His face changed subtly as he glanced at each one of us on his way back to his table. With Laney, his eyes widened a little like maybe he was daring her to say something else. With Tess, he remained neutral. And with me… he winked. He gave me a half-smile and subtle wink as if to say he didn't care about the marriage thing if I didn't.

Albert turned his back to us and walked away after that, and Laney let out a frustrated groan. "Did he *wink* at you just now?" she asked.

Tess laughed as she took a sip of her iced tea. "You were mad," she said to Laney.

"He's lucky that's all I said to him," Laney replied. "I almost tossed my drink at him to get him out of here."

I felt warm, fuzzy feelings about Laney being so protective. She was doing that for Daniel, being a protective sister, guarding me ferociously for his sake. I loved her for it. It made me happy that Daniel had a sister who loved him so much.

"I'm glad I didn't toss my drink," she said, shaking her head smiling at the thought.

"Why?" I asked. "Because you would feel bad about losing your temper?"

"No, because we would have had to clean everything up. He'd probably still be over here right now if I did that."

We were still laughing at that when Shannon walked up to take our order. She brought over some bread, and we all took a piece out of the basket and started eating.

"Daniel told me he taught you the military alphabet," Laney said a minute later.

"Oh yeah," I said. "That's cool."

"What is it?" Tess asked.

"You know, like that code they use in the Army for the alphabet. It's not a secret or anything. It's just the first letter of the word is the corresponding letter. You know, like A is alpha, B is bravo…"

"What's C?" Tess asked.

"Charlie," I said.

"What's T?"

"Tango."

"Tango? That's cool."

"Do you know them all?" Laney asked.

"I think," I said. "Mostly. I might get mixed up on a couple of them."

"What if you saw some of the words, like, written out on a piece of paper," Laney said. "Could you decipher the code?"

"Yeah, for sure," I said, with a shrug. "It's just the first letter. If you gave me letters and asked me to tell you their corresponding words, I might get mixed up. Like, I couldn't tell you what M is right now, but I know R is Romeo. That one stuck with me. S is Sierra."

"Huh," Tess said. "I thought it'd be Sam."

"What about this?" Laney asked.

She pulled a small piece of paper out of her purse and smacked it down on the table between us.

"What's this?" Tess asked.

I leaned in and picked it up. Laney had words scribbled on the page in sentence form. I read it out loud.

"India alpha mike hotel echo romeo echo." It was the end of the sentence, but I read, "*Echo, Romeo, echoooo!*" again in a distant, echo-sounding voice.

"Echo-Romeo-echo sounds cool," Tess said.

"Echo is a cool one in general," I agreed, nodding. "I said that to Daniel when he first taught me these. I like that one."

"Are you even going to see what it says?" Laney asked.

I focused on the page again, grinning at myself for getting distracted. *Echo is a cool one, though*, I thought as I stared down at the start of the sentence.

I began to focus on deciphering the code.

"I—A—M—H—E—R—E," I spelled it out loud, reading the first letter of each letter.

My head snapped up to look at Laney.

"Who wrote this?" I asked.

"Your husband," she said.

I gasped. I felt a physical jolt of pure joy and excitement. "Where is he?"

"He'll be here any second. I called him when I went to the restroom. He was at the hardware store. I thought he would have walked in by now. I was going to give you the note when I saw him come in. That's why I was trying to get Albert out of here."

My eyes watered. They were instantly glued to the door. I was antsy, squirming in my seat, and full of nervous energy.

"He said he got off the phone with you last night and hung up and drove straight here. He drove all night. He got here at like seven this morning and he slept until a few minutes ago." Laney was talking, and I was listening, but I did not take my eyes off the door of that restaurant.

"Of go," I said absentmindedly.

"What?" Laney asked.

"You said he slept until a few minutes ago, and I was thinking about this little boy in my class last year who thought the word *ago* was *of go*. He would say an hour *of go*, or a long time *of go*. It was really cute. How long did Daniel say he'd be?" I asked more urgently.

I was desperate enough for Laney's answer that I took my eyes off of the door and glanced at her. She looked uncertain, and I stood up.

"I'm just going to wait outside," I said, unable to take it any longer.

I got up, walked through the restaurant, and out through the front door. I saw Daniel in the parking lot, getting out of his truck. I ran to him. I locked eyes with Daniel as he stepped out of his truck, and I ran straight into his arms. I collided with him in the parking lot.

It had been a month since I had seen him, and even then, it was only for a day. I missed him so much it hurt. I was so excited that I was physically numb as I smacked into him. He cracked up as he caught me. I wrapped my legs around him, holding onto him, forcing him to hold me. He continued to laugh as he situated me, holding me, kissing me.

"Hello to you, too," he said.

I held his big face in my hands, kissing him, checking him out, unable to stop loving on him. "Hello, my best man. How did you end up here with me?"

"You said you wished I could come see the house."

"So, you showed up?" I asked, amazed. I kissed him again and again.

"I did," he said, smiling, kissing me back.

I was on the verge of melting on account of his smile and the taste of his lips. "I miss yooooou," I said. I knew he couldn't stand there and hold me in the parking lot, so I hopped to my feet after several long seconds. This made me shorter than him, and the first thing I did was stretch up and kiss him again. I could not leave him alone. I was starving for him.

"How long can you stay?" I asked.

"I have to head back tomorrow," he said. "Unfortunately. But it was a stretch for me to get here, even for that long."

"That gives us the rest of the day today, unless you need to sleep some more."

"No, I'm fine."

"We'll go look at the house, and then we have the rest of the day. What should we do?"

"Go to the beach," he said without hesitation.

And that was what we did. We saw the house, we loved it, and we called Evelyn and told her we wanted to buy it.

It was a gorgeous early summer day, and we took a quilt to the beach and spent our entire afternoon lying on the soft, dry sand. We watched people come and go. We talked to a few of them, but mostly, we just stretched out next to each other, breathing salty air, watching people, watching seagulls, talking, kissing, laughing, and being quiet.

Daniel and I were always touching. Most of the time, I was stretched out beside him. Some of the time we laid in the sun, and part of the time, the shadow of some palm trees fell on us and we were in the shade.

Neither of us felt bad about not spending time with family that day. We needed that afternoon together to reconnect and stoke the fire of our relationship.

It didn't need much stoking, honestly.

It was pretty piping hot.

But stoking the fire was fun nonetheless, and it was a priceless afternoon spent on the beach with Daniel.

Epilogue

⌒

Nearly two years later
Spring, 1975

I got a job teaching kindergarten at a public school in Galveston, and I was in the process of wrapping up my second year. In general, I loved my job. My first year had been wonderful. I had a great group of kids. This group wasn't bad, but there were a few with challenging personalities or circumstances.

One little girl named Lucy had lost her parents in a car accident in the fall. She and her little brother had been in the custody of the state since then. In this one school year, Lucy had lost her parents and moved twice. She and her little brother were in their second foster situation, and this one was even worse than the first.

I had asked for a hearing with Child Protective Services after I noticed a change in Lucy's countenance. At first, I thought it was just the shock of losing her parents, but then it seemed like it was more about her living situation. I asked her a lot about what was going on in her life, and I got the idea that she and Phillip were in a neglectful situation. She also said the adults talked about splitting up her and her little brother.

I hated having a student going through such a hard time. I hadn't anticipated this part of being a teacher, and it made me rethink my whole profession. I wondered, as a result of this experience, how many times over the years I'd be heart-wrenched and up all night worrying over a student.

I had been the one to call Child Protective Services, and today we would have a hearing to see if she and Phillip could possibly be moved again. It was 4:30pm on a Thursday, and I was getting ready to go to CPS offices.

I liked Lucy's caseworker, I felt like she did have the children's best interest at heart. I wasn't dreading the meeting, necessarily, but I could think of about ten other things I'd rather be doing with my Thursday afternoon.

That car accident had changed the trajectory of Lucy's life, and I was a pivotal player in her existence, so I had no choice but to intervene. I had no other choice but to worry. She was such an adorable, sweet girl, and it was difficult to witness the chain of events during the last year.

"Where are you going?" Daniel asked, coming into our house as I was getting ready to leave. I was standing in the kitchen, drinking some water and getting my thoughts together.

"I'm glad you caught me," I said, stretching up to kiss him when he came up behind me to greet me.

"When are you leaving?"

"Two minutes."

He kissed me again.

I wore no lipstick because I knew he would be coming home and I knew this would happen. Daniel loved to kiss me on the lips. It never got old to him. I found that I quite liked it as well.

"I need to leave, but I waited, knowing you were on your way."

"Thank you," he said. He kissed me again. "I might be at the gym when you get back, depending on what time you finish."

I nodded. "I figured you'd be gone. I might ride by there on my way home."

"Is Lucy getting a new home?"

"Not yet. This meeting is about trying to get her out of that other one. But I got this, I won't cry. I like that lady, Lucinda, the social worker. I feel like she's trying to help them out."

Daniel turned me in his arms, holding me close to him, kissing my neck. I leaned just the right way, letting him gain better access.

"It's good that they have you and her looking out for them," he said, hugging me, snuggling up to me.

I nodded as I reached up and absentmindedly touched the side of his face. "I hope we can get it taken care of before summer rolls around. Because then she's just on break, staying home all day. And who knows who she'll have for a teacher next year. She could move school districts with the new family. I might not even be able to check on her."

I took a deep breath, reminding myself for the thousandth time that I was doing everything I could. I made a conscious effort to set aside my worry and transport myself get back into the moment with my husband. I let my hands roam over his arms and shoulders, flirting with him. He leaned toward me and kissed my cheek.

"Just get them and bring them here if you want to. That way you'll know they're being treated good."

"What do you mean, get them and bring them here?" I asked.

"You can bring them home if you want," he said. "It's up to you, but I'm okay with it."

"Do you mean for us to foster them?"

He shrugged. "Or just go ahead and raise them. Whatever you think. It's up to you. I just wanted to let you know it's okay with me."

I stared at Daniel. I blinked in disbelief. "Could we even raise a kid?"

He laughed. "I thought you said you wanted us to start trying to have one sometime soon."

"I do, but that's different. With that, you start from a baby and grow into it." I stared into space, thinking about Lucy. "I didn't even think about that," I said. "I didn't think we were ready to raise a six-year-old."

"Well, maybe we're not, but I bet we'd do better than that place she's at now. But like I said, it's up to you. You know what you can handle, and—"

"Yes." I cut Daniel off in the middle of his sentence. "If you think we can, then, yes, Daniel. I want to."

"Okay, well, tell the lady we're thinking about it. Tell her we need a day or two, but ask her if it's even an option, and, you know, find out where we start with the process if we decide to do it."

"Do you think they would give them to us?" I asked.

Daniel squeezed me, smiling. "I did earn the Congressional Medal of Honor," he said. "I'm pretty sure they'd give me any baby I want."

Daniel was extremely humble about his accomplishments. He said things like that because he knew I could tell he was joking. I loved it when he showed off for me. I squeezed him back.

"You know it's two, right? There's two of them. They come together."

"Yes, I do know that," he said, giving me an amused grin. "You talked about this family all year. I'm familiar with the fact that there's two kids."

"Do you think we can do it?" I asked.

"Yes," he said. His easy smile was so calm and irresistible.

I thought of the responsibility of caring for those children. In spite of it being a crazy idea, it didn't seem daunting to me. The thought of taking the uncertainty out of their futures made a lump form in my throat. I blinked at my husband, holding back tears.

"I'm not sure yet, but I think you might have just become a dad."

He smiled. "Maybe congratulations are in order, then."

"I think it's congratulations *to me.*"

"For maybe being a mom?"

"No. For having the best husband in the whole world."

"That was so sentimental," he said, teasing me.

"You make me that way," I said with a shrug.

"If I didn't know any better, Abigail, I'd think you had a crush on me." He shook his head, pretending to be serious.

I smiled at Daniel and leaned up for a kiss, thinking he had no idea how severe this crush of mine was.

The End
(till book 3)

Other titles available from Brooke St. James:

Another Shot:
(A Modern-Day Ruth and Boaz Story)

When Lightning Strikes

Something of a Storm (All in Good Time #1)
Someone Someday (All in Good Time #2)

Finally My Forever (Meant for Me #1)
Finally My Heart's Desire (Meant for Me #2)
Finally My Happy Ending (Meant for Me #3)

Shot by Cupid's Arrow

Dreams of Us

Meet Me in Myrtle Beach (Hunt Family #1)
Kiss Me in Carolina (Hunt Family #2)
California's Calling (Hunt Family #3)
Back to the Beach (Hunt Family #4)
It's About Time (Hunt Family #5)

Loved Bayou (Martin Family #1)
Dear California (Martin Family #2)
My One Regret (Martin Family #3)
Broken and Beautiful (Martin Family #4)
Back to the Bayou (Martin Family #5)

Almost Christmas

JFK to Dublin (Shower & Shelter Artist Collective #1)
Not Your Average Joe (Shower & Shelter Artist Collective #2)
So Much for Boundaries (Shower & Shelter Artist Collective #3)
Suddenly Starstruck (Shower & Shelter Artist Collective #4)
Love Stung (Shower & Shelter Artist Collective #5)
My American Angel (Shower & Shelter Artist Collective #6)

Summer of '65 (Bishop Family #1)
Jesse's Girl (Bishop Family #2)
Maybe Memphis (Bishop Family #3)
So Happy Together (Bishop Family #4)
My Little Gypsy (Bishop Family #5)
Malibu by Moonlight (Bishop Family #6)
The Harder They Fall (Bishop Family #7)
Come Friday (Bishop Family #8)
Something Lovely (Bishop Family #9)

So This is Love (Miami Stories #1)
All In (Miami Stories #2)
Something Precious (Miami Stories #3)

The Suite Life (The Family Stone #1)
Feels Like Forever (The Family Stone #2)
Treat You Better (The Family Stone #3)
The Sweetheart of Summer Street (The Family Stone #4)
Out of Nowhere (The Family Stone #5)

Delicate Balance (Blair Brothers #1)
Cherished (Blair Brothers #2)
The Whole Story (Blair Brothers #3)
Dream Chaser (Blair Brothers #4)

Kiss & Tell (Novella) (Tanner Family #0)
Mischief & Mayhem (Tanner Family #1
Reckless & Wild (Tanner Family #2)
Heart & Soul (Tanner Family #3)
Me & Mister Everything (Tanner Family #4)
Through & Through (Tanner Family #5)
Lost & Found (Tanner Family #6)
Sparks & Embers (Tanner Family #7)
Young & Wild (Tanner Family #8)

Easy Does It (Bank Street Stories #1)
The Trouble with Crushes (Bank Street Stories #2)
A King for Christmas (Novella) (A Bank Street Christmas)
Diamonds Are Forever (Bank Street Stories #3)
Secret Rooms and Stolen Kisses (Bank Street Stories #4)
Feels Like Home (Bank Street Stories #5)
Just Like Romeo and Juliet (Bank Street Stories #6)
See You in Seattle (Bank Street Stories #7)
The Sweetest Thing (Bank Street Stories #8)
Back to Bank Street (Bank Street Stories #9)

Split Decision (How to Tame a Heartbreaker #1)
B-Side (How to Tame a Heartbreaker #2)

Cole for Christmas

Somewhere in Seattle (Alexander Family #1)

Thanks to my team ~ Chris, Coda, Jan, Glenda, Evette, and Pete

CPSIA information can be obtained
at www.ICGtesting.com
Printed in the USA
LVHW111315200722
723971LV00001B/3

9 781400 333004